MY Sugar DADDY

The Sugar Daddies Series Book One

#1 Amazon Best-Selling Romance Author

TRINITY BLACIO

My Sugar Daddy, Book One of the Sugar Daddies Series
Copyright © 2017 by Trinity Blacio

All Rights Reserved. No part of this book may be reproduced or transmitted in any form or by any means, electronic or mechanical, including photocopying, without permission in writing from the publisher.

This is a work of fiction. Names, characters, places and incidents are the product of the author's imagination or are used fictitiously. Any resemblance to actual events, locales or persons, living or dead, is coincidental.

For more information contact:
Riverdale Avenue Books
5676 Riverdale Avenue
Riverdale, NY 10471
www.riverdaleavebooks.com

Design by www.formatting4U.com
Cover by Scott Carpenter
Digital ISBN: 978-1-62601-357-5
Print ISBN: 978-1-62601-358-2
First Edition published by Ellora's Cave, 2015
Second edition, March 2017

Chapter One

Laura McGill stared at the website page again before turning to pull the blanket over her son Max. Her friend Carmen had let it slip last night at work that she now had a sugar daddy helping her with her college tuition.

She'd been shocked. First, because Carmen's figure was similar to hers—full and plentiful. Second, she never thought her friend had the balls to do anything like that.

Carmen had just gone from full-time to part-time at the diner, so Laura now received more hours at work and more tips, but it also meant she had to be away from her son more. If only she could have found a position as a personal assistant, something she was trained for.

She began surfing the internet. She opened two sites that looked promising. One was clearly labeled 'Sugar Daddies', and the other, 'Big Beautiful Women'.

Of the two, *SugarDaddies.com* seemed sleazier than the one for Big Beautiful Women. The BBW site was beautifully done, with sensual pictures of plus-sized women in different positions. The front photo on the page captured her attention, so she clicked the other site closed.

Big Beautiful Women is a website for servicemen. We're looking for that special lady. You will be spoiled and cared for. Do you dare take the chance and register? Who knows what is beyond that next click?

Slowly Laura took in her surroundings. Huge cracks ran down the walls of her apartment, and the heat barely worked. Last night she'd seen a rat the size of a small cat in the hallway of her building. If they were in the complex, more than likely the little monsters were everywhere.

There was no other choice. She needed help, and needed it now. Laura would not risk her son's health or life no matter what it cost.

What does it matter anyway? It's not as if I'm a virgin. She took another peek at Max, the only good thing in her life.

Her son's father, Warren Brunks, was not. He was a football coach for Grant High School and she found out after the fact that he was married. He'd denied Max was his since his birth and his wife made sure Laura's life was hell.

When they say the rich get away with things smaller men and women couldn't even contemplate, they weren't kidding. Born with a silver spoon in her mouth, Warren's wife would not listen to reason. Laura was the slut who was trying to ruin her so-called perfect marriage.

Not only had they gotten Laura fired from her job, emotionally she'd been treated like the scum of the earth. The threatening letters started first, followed by slashed tires and rotten food thrown onto her porch.

My Sugar Daddy

Warren's wife had accomplished what she'd threatened to do—she'd run Laura out of town. After losing her job, Laura had packed her bags and moved back to her hometown, Elyria, Ohio, using the last of the money she'd saved over the years. Elyria was thankfully more than 200 miles from her lying ex and his crazy wife.

Shaking off the memory, Laura continued to fill out the form; butterflies dancing in her stomach as she did so.

Single, check. Female seeking male, check. Bra size, 42 DD, Weight, 220. *Hmm, should I put my real weight? Well, they're going to see me, so why not?*

She continued to the next page and sat there, stunned.

Please mark what you would consider. *Damn, I don't know what half of these are.* She contemplated a few of the options such as Ménage and two or more men.

She fanned herself with her hand and sat back, zoning out a little. The thought of two or more men touching and loving her had never entered her mind. Hell, one was trouble enough, but the thought of two or more sent a chill up her back and had her checking it off as a 'will-try.'

Twenty minutes later Laura, hovering the mouse over the enter button, hesitant with nervous excitement, sent her information. "Well, it's done. Let's see who they match me up with." She got up and grabbed a cup of coffee. She'd truly missed coffee during her pregnancy, but she'd missed her mother more.

"I miss you, Momma." She took a sip of her coffee, staring at the picture of her mom on the wall

Trinity Blacio

above the kitchen table. Laura had her mother's same eye color, hazel, along with her body type, full-figured.

Her mom had been small and round but she was a powerhouse. Cross her or hurt her daughter and she'd come after you with a baseball bat. Laura smiled and remembered the time when a boy had come to pick her up for a date.

Before her mother had answered the door, she'd placed a baseball bat in the corner of the hall, making sure anyone who stepped into the house saw it. Of course, Laura had been furious and rolled her eyes, making her date laugh, but her mom wouldn't back down when it came to protecting her baby. It was still so hard to believe a year and two months had passed since she had lost her mother to cancer.

Making her way back to the computer, Laura thought of all the changes that had taken place in the last year. Her life had taken a spiral downward until the birth of her child. The first moment she'd seen Max, something clicked inside her. Laura was bound and determined to make a life for them, just as her mother had made one for her when her father walked out on them.

Although she was never one for feeling sorry for herself or dwelling on the negative aspects of her life, Laura still prayed the local karma bus would make a special visit to Warren and his wife.

Laura had been pregnant with Max at the time of her mother's death, but she'd made sure to keep all aspects of her private life from her mother. The added stress would not have done her any good, and she wanted her mother's last days to be happy.

My Sugar Daddy

Her computer pinged to tell her she had email. The site had found matches for her.

"So, it begins," she whispered.

* * *

Daniel Wilmot tapped his fingers on his desk and stared at the information on the webpage. There was something about the woman's profile that had his insides in knots. He never ignored the signals his body gave him. It had saved his life—and those of his comrades—plenty of times. He sent his request to communicate with her.

At the age of 40, Daniel—along with his brothers—set this website up for two purposes. One, to attract a certain type of woman for the many servicemen under their care. The second, a warning broadcast system for his Special Forces unit. Badger Broadcasting Warning or Big Beautiful Women both equaled *BBW.com* and no one was the wiser.

He and his brothers were also members of an elite team of men called the Badgers. Comprising warriors who had served in the U.S. military, the Badgers were 100 trained killers who were under the command of Grant Wilmot. They went where no others could go—or wanted to. Each man brought a hidden talent to the team, something even most of the highest-ranking officials knew nothing about. Only the president, the Joint Chiefs of Staff and his brother, Grant, had access to their unit.

The front of a sugar-daddy site worked well. Over the past three years, four men had found their special ladies while also warning many of their soldiers of threats in their respective areas of the world.

Badger men, for the most part, requested full-figured women. With their special abilities, strength and size, many team members—including himself—wouldn't dare touch a smaller woman. In part because they were afraid they'd hurt the women—but also because of their personal tastes. They wanted someone who could handle their rough loving, the BDSM aspects they all practiced, and they wanted a woman who could cope with their often-dangerous lifestyles.

Even though they allowed some men other than those on their team on the website, Daniel made sure none would abuse the females who applied.

Daniel had retired at 38 from the Marines' Force Recon team, and the high-level clearance he had made it easy to run background checks on anyone they needed, or wanted to. Even before he ran a check on this woman, Daniel let caution escape him and emailed his profile to her while he ran her data through his other computer.

He adjusted his cock as he read her description and waited. Laura McGill was five- foot-five and her measurements made his mouth water. At 6'4", his bulk had scared more than a few women away. It was one of the reasons he preferred plump women.

He and his brothers were always careful who they dated. Their family name alone brought out the gold diggers and sluts looking to land one of the Wilmot brothers.

He leaned back in his chair and looked out at the New York skyline. Yes, he and his brothers had been born into a family of wealth, but each son had made his own fortune by the age of 30.

When the first Wilmot—his great-grandfather Andrew Wilmot—came to America in the early 20th century, he'd had only a few dollars to his name. All that changed when Andrew and his son opened their winery. With the first batch of wine, jellies and other homemade juices, their reputation for excellence was established.

Like his grandfather, Daniel's father had built his own empire in real estate while keeping their family's vineyards going. Following in their footsteps, Daniel had made his money in stocks and computers. Daniel's older brother Grant, in the next office over, had kept pretty much to himself after coming back from Afghanistan. The Army had sent Grant on a recon mission that had changed his life.

Every one of Daniel's five brothers had served in their country in some way, driving his mother crazy. He smiled, remembering his homecoming. Both his mother and his sister hugged him, then yelled at him for scaring them.

Glancing at the door that connected his office and Grant's, Daniel frowned, worried about his brother. Grant had come back withdrawn, often locking himself in either his office or his home. His father had taken Daniel aside and asked him to keep an eye on Grant.

Maybe this beauty, Laura, would bring Grant out of his shell. They hadn't shared a woman since he'd come back, but it was time to change that—and he had a feeling she would be the partner they both needed.

The beeping of the fax machine drew Daniel's attention—here was her life history on three sheets of paper. He reached for the first sheet and smiled at the picture. Big hazel eyes stared at him—but the child she was holding surprised him.

Daniel grabbed the next page. What he read made him furious. He glanced to the picture again. So, the dad had denied all claims to the child. Something just didn't sound right—and he'd find out what.

"Daniel, do you have the Manner file?" Grant came into the room and looked at him.

"On the corner of the desk. Have you heard of the last name Brunks?" It was sticking to him like he should know it, but he couldn't grasp the memory.

His brother snorted. "Asshole. You *should* remember it. It was the only time you actually got suspended from Riverdale." Grant snatched the file and leaned over the desk, looking at the picture of Laura.

"Who's the woman?" Grant asked.

Smiling, Daniel sat back in his seat. "She's going to be ours. Her name is Laura McGill."

"She might be yours, but I don't need anyone!" Grant stormed out of the room and slammed the connecting doors, locking them behind.

In college, Grant and Daniel had been drawn to the same women and had enjoyed sharing them. The last time they had shared a woman had been right before Grant deployed.

They'd talked about finding the perfect woman, but lately every time Daniel brought up the subject his brother ignored him.

But Grant couldn't hide his interest when he'd glanced at the photo. Oh yes, Laura would be theirs.

"You just sealed your fate, big brother." He laughed and started to plan.

Chapter Two

Laura rested her feet in a tub of hot water as she fed her son. She'd pulled a double shift waiting tables. The blisters from the new shoes had burst open, but at least the rent would be paid next month.

Tomorrow she would go grocery shopping and pick up a paper. They couldn't live in this dump anymore. She'd seen another rat and this one was bigger than the last one.

We have $2000 left in the bank. I was trying to save, but it looks as if we'll have to use it for a deposit on a new place. Laura rested her head on the sofa.

It had been two weeks since she'd applied for a sugar daddy and Laura had been corresponding with one man. Hell, the only man she'd gotten a response from. He seemed nice enough, but was she actually ready to meet him? Did she really know enough about him?

It was a little late to debate this since she had agreed to meet him in less than two hours.

Each day he'd asked her a set of strange questions. She smiled and remembered the last set sent. *What is your idea of a relaxing day? When did you lose your virginity? What is your favorite color and beverage? If you had a choice to live anywhere in the world, where would it be? Do you have any animals? What sexual toys have you ever used?*

He most likely considered her boring after reading her answers. Laura's idea of relaxing was sipping a glass of red wine while curled up on the sofa with a book. Her favorite color was red; her favorite beverage, coffee. She'd taken some time to think of places in the world, but when it came down to it, her favorite place to live was where she'd been born—Elyria, Ohio.

She knew it was a small town no one had really heard of, but it was where happy memories outweighed everything else—the picnics at the park, going to the mall with her friends and just hanging out with her mom. She needed to make a trip back there, and soon.

Laura answered the rest of the questions. She had a few toys. A butt plug—which she still hadn't had the nerve to try—and two different dildos. Losing her virginity to that bastard Warren was what stung the most. Laura had gone without for so long, wanting to wait for the right man. She'd believed when she met him, she'd know—but Warren and his false sweet-talking took that gift away.

She still couldn't believe the man she was corresponding with was one of the wealthiest men in Manhattan, but Laura had done her homework. Trust was a big issue with her now and she was not going to be screwed again.

The pictures she'd seen of him were enough to make her wet. His size was a little scary, but she so loved a big man. There wasn't any lack of sexual

My Sugar Daddy

attraction, but she also wanted to make sure he knew all about her baby.

There would be no lies, even if this ended up being just a sexual thing.

She put the bottle down and started to burp Max. "We're going on a little outing Max, but not to worry, you can sleep the whole time in your stroller."

Glancing at her laptop, she frowned. *I just wish those stupid spam letters would stop popping up on my screen.* She'd scanned her PC three times; everything appeared normal.

Her son let out a little burp. She smiled as she changed him and put him in his best little outfit. Afterward, she tucked him into the stroller and got ready for their trip to the local coffee shop. *He must have women in every state. Why would he want to come to Ohio?*

Laura made her way to the bathroom—she had about an hour before she needed to meet Daniel. She stripped and climbed into the shower, turning on the hot water, wishing she had time to soak in a hot tub instead. She was a little nervous, but she needed help and if going out with this gentleman meant she could help Max, then so be it.

As she washed the smell of food off her body, she thought about Daniel's personality. Just from his emails she knew he was very assertive. He could dominate her body, but when it came to her son and her life, no one would catch her off guard again. If he wanted to play, why not? As long as she got what she needed out of the relationship.

Stepping out of the shower, Laura dried herself and wrapped the towel around her long hair. Today she would just put it back in a braid. There was no sense in getting all dressed up. If Daniel wanted to see the real her, he would.

Considering herself in the mirror, she traced over the small scar on her belly. *Max.* She'd had to have a C-section since he was so big. At 13 pounds, he'd been the biggest baby born in Elyria in a while. Laura stepped into the boxer briefs she loved to wear and grabbed a bra.

It had taken her a long time to find a place selling plus-sized women's things that didn't look like granny clothes. The extra cost was worth it, though. She looked at herself in the mirror. *Not bad, even for a big woman.*

Spraying herself with her favorite Mary Kay body spray, she rubbed her arms together to distribute the fragrance. Laura reached for her jeans and stepped into them before putting on her sweater.

She laughed when she saw the clock. It took her a total of 15 minutes to get ready—unlike her best friend, who usually took a good hour.

Twenty minutes later, Laura and Max made their way down the street. She spotted Daniel sitting at one of the outside tables of the coffee shop. His hair was in a military cut and his shoulders were wide. A black T-shirt covered his massive chest and she noticed his black jeans hugging his sculpted thighs when he rose to greet her.

Holding out his hand, he accepted her smaller one. She was shocked when he brought it up to his mouth and kissed her palm.

"It's a pleasure to meet you Laura. May I?" He looked to the stroller and at once she stiffened, but nodded.

My Sugar Daddy

"Daniel, this is my son, Max McGill." She picked up her cooing son and sat down in the seat Daniel had pulled out for her.

"He's a big boy. How old is he, and may I?" Daniel asked, holding out his hands.

"He's four months old. Max was big at birth; over 13 pounds—one of the reasons I had to have a C-section with him."

She watched as Daniel took her son into his arms and cradled him against his chest, as if he'd held children before. She relaxed a little seeing how comfortable he was with a child in his arms.

"What a handsome little man. And he has your eyes," said Daniel.

Daniel noticed the minute she relaxed—seeing how he'd handled her son. A waiter came out and served them two coffees and a desert; Daniel had already ordered.

"I hope you don't mind. The flavor of the week sounded so sinful, and who can turn down carrot cake?" He placed Max back in the stroller and sat down.

"Not at all. I figured you were the kind of man to take charge." She looked around, then leaned forward. "I was hoping you'd pick this. I stopped by last night after work to see what the specials were going to be. I happen to love carrot cake and when I heard the coffee of the day would be double-chocolate mousse I couldn't resist." She took a sip of her coffee, her lips twitched and he lost it.

He threw his head back and laughed so hard he thought he would pop the button on his jeans. She smiled, took a small bite of her carrot cake and moaned. Her small tongue came out where she proceeded to lick the top of her lip, wiping away the dot of cream-cheese frosting.

His cock hardened and rubbed against his zipper. "You, my dear, need to be turned over my lap and spanked." He took her hand and squeezed it.

"You played me, and for that alone I could make that cute ass of yours red, but if you keep licking those lips I'm going to…" He was interrupted when her cell phone rang.

"I'm sorry. There are only three people who have this number." Laura frowned and dug out the small, cheap phone. "Mrs. Cutter, what's wrong?"

She mouthed the word "babysitter" and he nodded, taking a sip of his coffee. He scanned the surroundings, a habit he'd learned overseas. His rental truck was parked across the street where he could see it. He didn't like her living in this neighborhood at all. He'd soon take care of that.

"What do you mean she called you? How do you know her?" Laura's voice rose and he turned his attention on her, seeing that she was stiff and upset.

"I should have known you were too good to be true. Tell me, did you take my son to see the bitch?" She shut the phone and took three deep breaths before turning the phone off.

"What is it, Laura? How can I help?" He reached over and took her hand. She was trembling and when she looked up at him there were tears in her eyes.

"Seems the father of my son wants to talk with me. He and his wife both do. So, unless you know of a good and cheap lawyer, there is nothing you can do for me. So much for a new apartment. If you'll excuse me,

My Sugar Daddy

I need to go home." She started to rise but he held onto her hand.

"As a matter of fact, I do know a good lawyer. Finish your cake and coffee while I make a call." He knew she would have a hard time eating but it gave her something to do while he called his brother Grant.

It looked as if Daniel didn't need to think of a reason to bring the two of them together. Once he heard about her problem, he'd be there in a second.

He dialed Grant's cell number, hoping he was done with his business in Cleveland. The only reason Grant had come was to finish the deal about the hotel they were constructing.

"What?" Grant snapped.

"Are you done? I need your assistance now," Daniel snapped back, not in the mood for one of his brother's outbursts. Daniel leaned forward and growled into the phone.

"This isn't for me. Laura needs a lawyer and I know you're the best, but if you don't want to help the woman out, fine, we'll find someone else to protect her son." Laura gasped and he reached under the table, squeezing her knee.

"Where do you want me to meet you?" his brother asked.

Daniel handed Laura the phone. "Give my brother your address and he'll meet us there."

She hesitated for a minute and shook her head. "I can't ask that of you or him." She smiled and leaned over, cupping his cheek. "You're a special man. You need to find someone who is right for you. Not someone who has a ton of problems."

Taking the phone, she stood. "Thank you and I'm

sorry your brother disturbed you, but really, we'll be fine." She closed the phone and placed it on the table before she turned to leave. "Oh, and you might want to check your computer for viruses. Every time you sent me an email some sort of spam would pop up on mine." Laura tucked the blanket around Max, smiling down at him.

Daniel's phone rang. The song *Bad to the Bone* played, indicating his brother was calling. He opened it and said, "Four three five six seven Fir Ave. We'll be waiting." He stood and hooked his arm around her waist after he threw a $20 onto the table, nodding to the waiter.

"Let's go." She tried to slip out of his grasp, but he held onto her and turned her in his arms. "Stop. I'm not going anywhere. We're going to help you and you're going to let us. Think of your son. Do you want this man to take him?" He hated to use that card, but she needed them and he wasn't about to let her go.

Her shoulders slumped and she sighed. "No but I can't repay this. All you wanted was someone to have sex with. Why are you doing this?" Confused and hurt, Laura allowed him to guide them to his truck.

"Take the baby and get in the truck. I'll put the stroller in the back. We'll discuss this when we get to your place, but Laura…" He rested his hand on her shoulder. "I know everything. Do you really think I wouldn't have run a background check?"

She shrugged and held onto her son. "I have nothing to hide. All you had to do was ask, but I guess with your money, I can't blame you. You are not the only one who did some checking." With that, she slid into the seat and rocked Max.

Daniel couldn't wait to get his hands around Warren's scrawny neck.

He'd thought seeing Laura would lessen what he'd felt when he stared at her picture, but it hadn't. One look at her and Daniel knew she was the one for them.

He kept his clenched hands at his sides, but with her curves and that little dimple on her left cheek, all he wanted to do was touch her.

Now all he had to do was convince her and his brother they were perfect together and try not to land in jail for murdering Warren.

Easy.

Chapter Three

Laura placed Max in his crib and turned on the baby monitor before leaving his room. He'd fallen asleep in her arms on the short ride back to the apartment. As soon as she stepped into their small apartment, her landline rang and she'd grabbed it before it could wake Max.

"We're on our way there, slut," Warren barked. He hung up before she could say a word.

Her life was falling apart and she didn't know where to turn. A stranger stood in her living room waiting for her and offering his help, but at what cost? She looked into the bathroom mirror and sighed. She had no choice. Turning on the faucet, she splashed water on her face and kicked off her shoes.

Once everyone left, Laura would break down, but right now she needed to pull up her big-girl panties, as her grandmother used to say.

Laura heard the knocking at the door, grabbed the towel and dried her face. Daniel stood by the window and watched every move she made as she answered the door. A man, taller than Daniel, filled her doorway. He had black hair and a mustache, but what caught her attention were his deep-blue eyes. They were the same as Daniel's.

My Sugar Daddy

"Are you going to let me in or are you going to gawk at me some more?" He crossed his arms over his chest and stared at her.

"Excuse me? I wasn't gawking. I was admiring your eyes. They are the same as Daniel's. And if you can't be any nicer, then no, I'm not inviting you in. I have enough crap to deal with. I sure as hell don't need your attitude, whether you're an attorney or not!"

She went to slam the door in his face when his hand caught the door and he carefully pushed it back open. He slid a finger down her cheek and grinned down at her. "You've got spunk, that's for sure." He strolled into her apartment and shook his brother's hand before they both turned to stare at her.

"What is going on? I take it Warren Brunks is the one behind the trouble?" the man said before even introducing himself.

She let the front door slam shut and stared at both men. Taking a deep breath, she moved to the kitchen and grabbed three beers. Laura handed each of the men a beer and kept one for herself.

"My name is Laura McGill, and you are?" She opened her beer and curled up on the sofa, waiting.

"I'm Grant, the oldest of the Wilmot brothers, but then you already knew that." He sat down at the other end of the couch while Daniel set his beer on the table next to her and picked her up.

"What are you doing?" she asked as he set her on his lap, sitting where she had been.

"Isn't it obvious? Now tell my brother what he needs to know. What did the babysitter have to say and what is that snob Warren doing?"

Taking a sip of her beer, Laura sighed and leaned

back against Daniel. "I don't even know why you two are doing this. I can't pay you, Mr. Wilmot. I have a total of $2000 left in my savings from my mom, which I'd hoped to use to find a new place to live." She looked around.

"I can't stay here. I've seen rats in the hallway and I won't risk my son getting sick."

Grant took a gulp of his beer and rose off the couch and proceeded to look around her apartment. "The Carlton House?" he asked his brother, who nodded.

"For now," Daniel responded before turning his attention to her. "We have a three-bedroom condo open and it would be close to our offices." Daniel swirled his beer around before bringing it up to his mouth.

"You're bringing her into the downtown office?" Grant sat back down and studied her.

"Do you have experience working in an office?" he asked her, jarring her out of the trance she'd been in.

"I used to work for the school board in Boston as personal assistant to the president. I worked there for over five years. Before that, I worked at the North Center Law Firm for the senior partner, also as an assistant. Should have kept that job too but I was stupid. Other than that, waitress jobs in my hometown and doing the same now. Why?" She looked at Daniel and then at Grant.

"Our family owns a building in downtown New York. We have condos there and one of them is open. I want you to move into it. It has three bedrooms, plenty of security and it's clean. We also need a secretary. Our offices are right down the street and there is even

My Sugar Daddy

a nursery in the building for our employees, which would be perfect for Max. You could spend your lunch hour with him."

Daniel slid his hand under her shirt and rested it on her stomach, making her release the air in her lungs.

"Daniel, please tell me why you want to do this. Isn't this a little much, even for a sugar daddy? I don't want to get screwed over again. I have a son to think about. I've heard of that place. It must be at least a $1,000,000 to rent it. Your family isn't going to want someone like me in one of their buildings."

She pushed his hand away and got up, going to the big window and concentrating on the apartment across the street. "Both of you know that even if I worked for you, it wouldn't be enough to cover the rent and utilities in a place like that."

Grant moved to one side of her and Daniel the other. "What do you think a sugar daddy does? He takes care of his woman, and we're going to take care of you. This is our world and you belong in it with us. Daniel was right this time. You're special." Grant latched onto her braid and yanked it, making her head tilt. He leaned down and captured her lips with his.

* * *

Daniel was both relieved and hard as a rock. The way she responded to his brother's touch had him waiting for his turn. Grant finally saw what he did in Laura. The beauty outside as well as inside, she was all woman and needing their loving. Her nipples were hard and he loved the little moan Laura made.

Her breasts were full and round and Daniel

couldn't help cupping each and running his fingers over her nipples. Laura moaned around his brother's kiss. He only hoped when the time was right she would accept them as they were.

Grant released her, but not before he squeezed her butt cheek.

She'd stiffened and had been on the verge of saying something when Grant kissed her, but right now she stood in between them, touching her swollen lips. Her nipples hard as pebbles Daniel lowered his head and sucked one into his mouth shirt and all.

Squirming, Laura retreated and they allowed it for now. "Umm, let me get this straight. You're both going to, we're going to…?"

Daniel turned her toward him and cupped her face in his hands. "My brother and I have always shared, since college. We've been searching for the right woman and I believe you're her. Eventually I'm hoping for more than a sugar-daddy relationship, as my brother has so rudely pointed out. However, I know it will take time for all of us to get to know each other but, yes, we will take care of you. The money you earn working for us at the office will be yours to keep. The condo and the car we give you will be our responsibility. You are not to worry about anything." Daniel let that settle in and kissed her lips softly.

"Let me describe what we want. While we are with you there will be no clothes, unless we say you need them. I want to see all of you; your curves when you walk, sit or bend. The way your muscles pull when stretched over a piece of furniture, waiting for whatever we give you." Daniel squeezed her breast while Grant moved in behind Laura and cupped her ass.

My Sugar Daddy

"I can't wait to see you bound, your arms stretched above you while your legs are wide open for our inspection. You won't be lying down when we do this. You'll be in the middle of the living room. Maybe we'll even leave the blinds open for anyone who wants to see, to watch as we touch what belongs to us. Will you belong to us, Laura? Do you have the courage to accept our terms?" Daniel asked and kissed her cheek at the same time he pinched her nipple.

She licked her bottom lip. He leaned over and nipped it. "Answer the question, Laura. Will you allow us to take care of you?"

The pounding on the door had her stiffening in their arms and jumping to stare at the door.

She jerked away from them and took a deep breath as she wiped her hands on her jeans, staring at the door.

"They're here. Warren and his wife." She looked over her shoulder at him, then at Grant. "Please don't let them take Max." Laura was so terrified Warren would take Max away she'd forgotten what they had just proposed.

Moving to the door before she could answer it, Grant frowned at her. "I do this because I want to. This has nothing to do with our deal. Every mother should have her child. I won't let him take yours away. You need to decide if you want us because you feel something here." He placed his hand over her heart and kissed the top of her head.

"He won't take your baby," he declared again before he threw open the door with a thud.

"What do you want?" Grant snarled at Warren and his wife. He was a man on a mission, and it seemed Laura was now his next assignment. The old Grant was making his way back, thanks to the beautiful woman in the middle of the room.

Laura bit her bottom lip, her eyes wide, and wiped her hands on her jeans again. She kept looking back and forth from the bedroom to the door.

Daniel slid his arm around her waist and kissed the top of her head. "It's okay. My brother will take care of this. Why don't you go check on your son?" He gave her a little push and she stared once more at the door, where Warren and his wife still stood.

"Go on. We'll take care of this. I promise." Laura didn't say a word and went into the bedroom. He knew she would listen but right now he didn't want her in the room.

He turned to glare at Warren.

"That slut needs to get back here. I need her signature on this paper," Warren's wife yelled and tried to push around Grant, but he wasn't having any of it.

"Excuse me, who are you?" Grant snatched the paper out of the woman's hand and started reading it.

The woman's mouth dropped open. For a few seconds she just stood there before straightening her shoulders and pulling down her shirt. "I'm Belinda Codell-Brunks, and you are?"

"He's my older brother, Grant Wilmot, and Laura McGill's personal attorney. Hello Warren, how's the nose? I still see the little bump never went away. Too bad it doesn't add character," Daniel drawled, leaning against the door and waiting for Grant to finish reading.

"I see Warren isn't the only one slumming. What,

is the bitch doing both of you for your help?" the woman sneered, eyeing him and then Grant.

"I guess the rumors were right," Grant said. "The Codells' daughter is a bitch and a snob. Glad Mom and Dad don't associate with them. Have Laura sign it. He's giving all paternal rights away. I'll want copies of this sent to my office." He handed Warren his card.

Next, he addressed Belinda. "When this is done, you will not contact her again. If I hear about you slandering her again, I'll have your skinny ass in court so fast you won't know what hit you."

When Grant moved to take the document to Laura, she was standing there with a pen in hand.

"I heard." She smiled and signed the paper, handing it back to Grant, who winked at her. "Oh, and Belinda? You can take that babysitter and shove her up your ass, right alongside Warren if there's room." She spun and disappeared around the corner into the kitchen.

"Here you go. Don't let the door hit you in the ass." Grant moved them toward the entrance and slammed the door in their faces as soon as they had the document in hand.

Chapter Four

Laura took a quick peek in the rearview mirror. Max was sound asleep in his car seat. She'd thanked both men and told them she needed time to think. Neither of them had wanted to leave, but she assured them both she would contact them by tomorrow, which was today.

The moment they left her apartment the crank calls started. First, no one would say anything. All she heard was a growl and then nothing. But this morning, the threats had started. Not only were they emailing her, now they were calling her and she had no idea how they'd gotten her phone number.

Calling out sick from work, Laura rushed to pack a bag for her and Max, heading straight to Elyria. She wanted to visit her mother's grave and her best friend, Alex. By the time she returned, maybe the calls would stop.

Before leaving her apartment, she'd called Alex, and her ear still rang from her squeal. Alex ordered her to come spend the night with her. And it had only taken Laura two seconds to agree.

She turned left into Brookdale Cemetery and followed the road all the way to the back. After she

My Sugar Daddy

parked her car, Laura sat there staring at the row of markers. Her mother's, the last one in the row, still had the flowers she'd sent last week.

"One year you've been gone, Momma." She opened her door, when her phone started to ring. She grabbed the phone and moaned when Daniel's number popped up on the screen. She'd been hoping to talk to them tonight, but it looked as if now was going to be the time.

"Afternoon, Daniel. I thought I was going to call you?" She sat on the edge of seat of the car, staring at her mother's stone.

"We stopped by your place to bring coffee and breakfast to find you gone. So we decided to wait for lunch and came back but you're still not here. Don't tell me we scared you off?" He sounded a little put out, but she didn't care. She'd made no promises and she needed time. What they wanted from her was big and affected not only her but her son as well.

"I needed to come home for a visit. I'll be staying with my best friend tonight and I was going to call you then. I'm sorry you went out of your way, but I did tell you both I need some time to think. You're asking me to move to a different state, Daniel, where I won't know anyone. What happens if you get tired of me and want me out of this apartment? I can't leave at a moment's notice, not with a baby. Give me tonight and I'll give you my answer tomorrow."

"Where are you?" he asked again with a little bite in his voice.

"I told you. I'm home." She looked at her phone and frowned.

"I'm standing in front of your home and you are

not there, Laura. I don't like to be lied to," Daniel informed her coldly.

She stood slowly, slamming her car door before opening her son's.

"For your information, you are standing at my apartment, not my home. And I don't lie. Goodbye, Daniel." She snapped the phone closed and turned it off.

"Sorry, Max. It looks as if we're once more looking at apartments. Maybe we'll look around here. It would be good to be around friends right now." She unhooked the car seat and took Max out of the car, placing him on the ground in front of her mother's headstone and sitting next to the car seat.

"Well, that problem is solved. Looks as if we won't be moving to New York. I'd so hoped they would be different." She started pulling at the weeds around her mother's grave.

"They both were really cute, Mom. The way they helped me with Warren was amazing." Laura sat back and sighed. "I should give them another shot since they did help me, but I'm tired of being hurt. How do I know they won't hurt me? And I have Max to think about too. I wish you were here."

A lone red-tail hawk circled above her head before it landed in front of her on her mother's headstone. It stared into her eyes, not moving. This wasn't the first time something like this happened to her. Some would say she had a gift.

"Okay, Momma. I'll give them one more shot, but if they hurt me I'm going to rip their balls off." She laughed when the bird flapped its wings and cried out before taking off.

My Sugar Daddy

"You were always one for show, but a hawk? Isn't that a little much, Mom?" She grinned, looking at her son, who was wide awake and following the bird with his gaze.

"Yep, that's your grandmother, Max. I wish you two could have met."

She dug out her phone and turned it back on. At once it rang and Daniel's number appeared again.

"I'll be back at the apartment at three tomorrow. I'll start packing then but tonight I'm staying with a friend," she said before he could say a word. "And Daniel, if you or

Grant ever accuse me of lying again, I won't hesitate to leave. I've never lied before and I won't start now."

"You are right and I'm sorry. What convinced you to move, if I may ask?" Daniel asked.

She straightened her legs out and looked up at the hawk. "I don't know if you'll believe me, but oh well. Let's just say my mom told me to go for it and my mother is never wrong." The hawk dipped down and landed on a grave marker two feet away from her. It stared at her son as it jumped to a closer stone.

"I thought your mother died last year," Daniel asked, sounding confused.

"Do you know how beautiful red-tail hawks are? It's rare for them to be so close to humans but one is visiting us at my mother's grave marker. Right now it's staring down at Max—quite an amazing sight. It's astonishing what spirits can do when they want to communicate."

On speakerphone, Grant looked at Daniel and frowned. "You're at your mother's gravesite and you have a hawk talking to you?"

He heard Laura's sigh into the phone. "No, Grant, the bird didn't talk to me and no I'm not crazy. My mother was a witch. Animals would come up to her naturally. She was one with Mother Nature herself. I have a little of her gift and I asked her about the both of you. I asked if I should give you a second shot. That is when the hawk appeared and landed on her headstone." She paused and he could hear her moving around.

"Do you still want me to move, even knowing I have this gift?" Laura asked as Daniel heard her say goodbye to her mother.

Both men stared out at the front of his truck, which was parked in front of her apartment building. A red-tail hawk had landed on the middle of his hood and was staring at them both. "Umm, Laura, it seems we have a visitor here on my hood," Daniel said into the speakerphone, shocked.

She laughed. "No wonder the hawk took off. Mom must have found a different animal. It's just my mother's way to let you know she's watching."

"Okay, we'll see you tomorrow, and Laura, be careful on the road please." Daniel said as they watched the bird stretch out its wings and scream before it took off again.

"Daniel…oh never mind. We'll be fine. I'll see you tomorrow." Laura disconnected the phone and he turned to his brother who shook his head.

"Don't even say it. We are not going to mention this again. Did you call Mike and have him turn on the utilities at the condo?"

He started the truck and pulled out onto the street heading toward their hotel. "Yes, it all will be ready

My Sugar Daddy

for her. Dad was there when I was talking with Mike. They want to meet Laura."

His brother moaned. "I don't know why they have to meet every woman we see. It's not as if we're ready to commit to anything yet."

Daniel snorted. "You are wrong there and you know it. There is something special with Laura. You're just afraid to admit it."

"Don't push it, Daniel. I agree she's beautiful and she'll be ours, but right now I can't promise anything more." His brother snapped and looked out the window.

"Do we have her medical records?" He asked as they pulled into the Marriott parking lot.

"Yes, and she is all clean. I'll call a moving company when we get upstairs and have them arrange to meet us there tomorrow. As far as her car goes, it's a junker and not safe. I'll have one of the local salvage places come and pick it up."

His phone rang as he parked the truck and Laura's phone number flashed on his phone. "Hello, Laura, something wrong?" Daniel sat in the truck turning on the speakerphone for his brother to listen also.

"I was putting my son in the car when I noticed another vehicle. Someone is following me and taking pictures. Could it be someone from the press? I mean, your family is very wealthy and I'm sure they are always looking to get the dirt on you. I thought the crank calls would stop if I left for a while and now this. I really don't want any publicity, Daniel, and my friend doesn't need it either." She paused and he heard her shifting gears before the cussing started on the phone.

31

"Stupid ass son-of-a-bitch! I don't care who you are, asshole. You don't cut me off and slow down, fuckwad," Laura screamed into the phone.

Daniel's gut tightened as he looked at his brother.

He too was staring at the phone between them. Grant shifted on his seat. "What's going on, Laura? Talk to us!"

"Whoever this is, he's smart. He's trying to make me stop but I've got a surprise for him. Did you know I use to race cars in high school with a bunch of my friends? Loved it! I'll have to check into it when we get to New York. Oh, no you didn't, dickhead. Why am I getting the feeling this is not the freaking press?" He heard the squeal of tires.

"Laura, don't stop, whatever you do. Go to the police station. Grant is going to call them now so they'll be waiting for you. What city are you in?" He started his truck, while Grant pulled out his phone and waited.

"Where do you think I'm trying to get to? Elyria. I'm sure not bringing this psycho to my friend's house." Once more he heard the grinding of her car's motor. "That's right, my car might look like shit, but you don't know what I've got underneath the hood, prick."

While Grant called the police, he programmed the GPS in the rental truck and at once started off on their journey. According to the GPS they had a four-hour trip ahead of them.

"Daniel, do you know who this is? He's not giving up! Shit!" She screamed as he heard a loud bang.

"What happened?" he yelled and turned onto the

highway. In the seat next to him, Grant was informing the local police what was happening.

"The asshole rammed the back of my car! Do you believe this shit? I hear sirens and I'm close to the police station right around the corner. He's turning down a street. He must know the city. I'm here at the station. Gotta go." She disconnected the phone and his heart sank.

"Hager! It has to be him." Daniel took a quick glance at Grant who nodded. A man they had considered a friend at one time, but found out later it all had been a ruse.

As one of the top ten terrorists in the world, Hager was a chameleon and a thorn in both his and Grant's sides. The thought of Laura being targeted by him had both men in military mode.

"If he's around, he'll be calling in the rest of his team—at least the ones who we haven't killed," his brother said, and dialed another number.

Daniel's stomach knotted and his old combat instincts kicked in. It seemed that Laura now had no choice. She would come with them no matter what if she and her son wanted to survive.

Chapter Five

Laura sat in the small cold room, her anger rising by the minute. Her son, thank God, had fallen asleep after she'd fed and changed him. She'd been stuck inside this room for the past three-and-a-half hours.

Oh, sure they'd brought her drinks, food and such, but they refused to say a word to her until six military men came into the room. They surrounded her and started asking all sorts of questions.

She squirmed in her seat, remembering how gorgeous they were.

Each of them reassured her they knew Daniel and Grant. That they were there to protect her and Max. But they turned around and left in ten minutes without another word. She stood and reached for the door, but jumped back as Daniel and Grant came into the room.

"Thank God you're okay," Daniel said and yanked her into his arms, almost crushing her ribs. Grant ran his hand down her back and squeezed her ass.

"You don't know how worried we've been, and I for one don't like to be worried." Daniel leaned down and kissed her cheek.

"Let go, Daniel." She pulled out of his arms and

My Sugar Daddy

glared at both men. "Now explain!" She tapped her foot and crossed her arms. "I want to get out of this room. I need to call my friend and tell her I'll be late. Your goons took my phone! Give it back." She held out her hand.

They each pulled out a chair and sat down as they shook their heads. "No phone. Sorry, but until we're out of here you will listen to every word we say." Daniel leaned forward, his elbows on his knees. He stared at her before reaching out and pulling her in between his legs.

"It's not just one man out there now, Laura. It's a whole team of specially trained men who've gone AWOL. They've centered their attention on you. I'm afraid they are trying to even the score with us. I can't tell you all of it since the information is only for high-clearance personnel, but the gist of it is we took out most of his team a few months back."

He slid his hands up her shirt and rested them on the bare skin of her back. "Grant and I are semi-retired special agents and right now our team is slowly coming together. I have three men right now at your friend's house. When the rest of our men arrive, we'll leave. Looks as if we'll be spending some time in one of our own safe houses." He lifted her shirt and leaned in, kissing her belly.

Grant reached over and pulled her out of Daniel's arms and into his lap. Laura slapped at his hands but he paid little attention as he arranged her legs so she straddled his lap. Her skirt, now pushed up to her stomach, exposed her panties and Laura knew they would see the wet spot on them.

She tried to get up but Grant held her hips. "Stay

put. We need to touch you and make sure you're okay. Hearing the crash when he rammed you put my stomach in my mouth."

He searched her eyes.

"Daniel was right, you're something special, and we won't lose you. We're in this for the long haul, Laura. I never believed in this first-sight crap and I know this is all too quick, but we'll get through it. This isn't the website or just sexual. We want all of you for however long we can get." He rubbed his cheek against her breasts and took a deep breath.

Shaking her head, Laura tried once more to get up but Daniel rose and came in behind her. He slid his hands under her shirt, pushing up her bra so he could cup her breasts. "Ours! You are ours, Laura and every chance we get we'll be demonstrating how much we need you and want you." He nipped the side of her neck and she moaned.

"You've got to stop. Anyone could walk in," she pleaded, but they didn't listen. Grant traced the edge of her panties before slipping his fingers underneath and pushing two fingers into her pussy.

"That excites you more, doesn't it, Laura? The thought of someone walking in while we touch and nibble on you? Tell me, what did you think of our men?" Grant asked, twisting his fingers inside her pussy as he pumped them in and out slowly. She could have sworn the door opened behind them, but Laura couldn't even think straight right now.

"Big. Please…" She had never been so turned on in her life. Cool air slipped over her now-exposed breasts.

"You're so beautiful. Your skin is flushed and I

can see your little nub all swollen and needing attention. Do you want to come, Laura?" Grant asked as Daniel slid over to her side and sucked one of her nipples into his mouth.

"So close, but not yet. Open your eyes, Laura," Grant ordered in a whisper, yet it was powerful enough that she opened her eyes.

She'd been right. Laura *had* heard the door earlier. Three of their men stood behind him, watching. They too were hard as rocks, if the outlines of their pants were any indicator. Laura's face heated as she turned her gaze back onto Grant.

She sucked in her breath, the same time Grant stroked her clit, sending her over the edge. "Come!"

Her scream was muffled when Daniel released her breast and covered her mouth with his. His kiss was hard and demanding. "Others will watch, but none will touch you unless we allow it. This pussy, this body, is ours now, Laura. Isn't it?" Grant asked and licked her other nipple as another fine tremor soared through her.

Daniel lifted his head a fraction, but held her chin in his grasp. "Tell us you're ours, that you want us as badly as we want you."

Her body hummed with sexual gratification, but could she really commit to these two men? "I don't know…" She buried her face into Grant's neck when Daniel released her and stood behind her.

"Shhh, we have plenty of time to convince you." Grant tucked her breasts back into her bra and lowered her shirt. She didn't look up.

"Are all the men here now, Seth?" Daniel asked.

"All but two," a deep baritone voice informed

him. A shiver ran up her spine and she peeked up to see to whom the voice belonged.

Grant laughed and nipped her ear. "Sorry. He can watch, but that's all. I've lost too many women to him."

The man in question had to be close to seven feet tall and was as black as the night. His biceps rippled when he laughed and he slapped Grant on the back lightly, so as not to jar Laura. "You two weren't serious about those women. I wouldn't do that to you with this one—she's a keeper. Treat her well, my friend." He winked at Laura.

"Or I'll personally come down and kick your ass," added the Hispanic gentleman with tattoos running up and down both arms. "My name is Zenith, pretty lady. Any time one of these dumbasses gives you trouble, you just call me and I'll make sure to thump on them." He leaned down and kissed the top of her head.

"Watch it, Sergeant!" Grant snapped. He stood and slowly lowered her to the ground and smiled down at her. "Just so you know, I'm the one who is in command here."

As soon as Grant said that, each man stiffened, and she was shoved behind Grant as the door to the room was thrown open with so much force it banged into the wall, scaring her son.

"Son of a bitch. I just got him to sleep, you idiot," Laura yelled at the person, not even looking up. She shoved through the wall of men to get to Max. "I don't know what is wrong with you but enough, I want to leave now!" She scooped her son into her arms.

"Shhh, Max, it's okay." Laura glared at the police

My Sugar Daddy

captain, Jeffery Bridge as he crossed his arms and glared back. She should have figured it would be the one dickhead who'd had a grudge on her since high school.

"If you don't want to know that your mother's grave has been dug up; her body stolen, or that your friend is missing, then please go." He swung his arm to the door. "You were always great at running."

All eyes turned to her but nothing mattered as she managed to fall into the chair behind her. Her mother's final resting place had been desecrated and her best friend was missing.

Anger, disbelief and hurt all swirled around her, but then she looked evenly into Jeff's eyes and said, "You know, Jeff, you were always a sore loser. And for your information, I didn't run. I walked away from your ass. Sorry, but I didn't date bullies then then and I don't now."

The room quieted down and Daniel and Grant kneeled before her. "Your friend isn't missing. She's been taken to a secured place, where three of my men are guarding her. As far as your mom, I'm sorry. I don't know why they did this but we'll find them-and—her." Grant kissed the top of her head and stood while Daniel rubbed Max's back too, trying to comfort them both.

"We'll be leaving now. But, Mr. Bridges, if you ever, and I mean *ever,* take that attitude with my woman again, you won't see another sunrise," Grant snarled. "I expect any news to be sent to my man, Seth. I will also be leaving two men here to help with the recovery of Laura's mother. She will be found and put to rest again."

Laura realized that up to this point, both men had only revealed their softer sides to her, but watching Grant deal with Jeff and his men, she now knew their strength.

She turned her attention to Daniel and saw the same expression on his brother's face. She'd known both men were the dominant type, but this was totally different.

"Why do I feel I'm just now seeing the real you?"

Chapter Six

Daniel looked back at Laura as they drove out of Elyria, heading toward their small private airport just outside of Cleveland. She hadn't said a word as they'd ushered her out to the waiting Hummer. Her belongings were packed in the back and Max was next to her. She hadn't cried or objected at all, just stared out the window.

Grant sat next to her while Seth drove. Zenith and Caser were behind them. Grant met his worried gaze and he nodded.

"So, tell us about this police captain. Did you date him in high school?" Grant scooted closer to her and wrapped his arm around her.

She looked at Grant, then at Daniel before turning to look out the window. "If you call one date going out. He tried something and I said no. He got angry, hit the wall and I left. End of story. Oh, he tried to get me to go out with him again, but I wouldn't and you saw his attitude this afternoon. He acted like an ass all throughout school. Is that enough information?" She tried to hide the grin but failed. Grant snarled and nipped her ear.

"You'll get my mother's body back, right? I know

she's not in her body, that she's watching us now, but it's just not right. Why would they do that to her?"

"There have been some rumors but we haven't been able to confirm anything yet." Daniel sighed. "We're not supposed to mention this but..." He looked to Grant and he nodded.

"Have you ever seen the TV show *The Walking Dead*? Think small scale on that end. We've found evidence they are very close to actually succeeding," Grant informed her as he brushed the hair away from her face.

"You're kidding, right? They're trying to make zombies? Why the hell would you do that?" She held up her hand. "Wait, forget I said that. I know why. Our government is doing the same thing, isn't it? They want to use them as weapons or something?" She took a deep breath.

"We don't know what our government is doing, and frankly I don't want to. The thought of this happening is mind-blowing. We have orders to stop them at any cost and we *will* stop them, Laura." Daniel reached back and squeezed her knee.

Grant stretched his legs out in front of him as much as he could and looked at Laura. "Do you still want to come back to New York with us, knowing we could take off anytime on a mission and that you and Max might have to be kept hidden for a while?"

"Grant, this can wait," Daniel said, his attention on Laura.

She turned in her seat. "And what if we get to this hiding place and you get sick of us? Do you know how much work and time a baby takes, Grant, Daniel? Do the both of you really want to be in our lives? You can't have just me. Max and I are a package deal." She reached over and tucked the baby's foot back in the car seat without waking him.

"I'll tell you what," Daniel said. "Why don't we use this time as a window of opportunity?" Laura looked up at him, then at Grant. "I take it we're going to be at this secret location for a while, so why not use this time as our trial period. The three of us can get to know the other's quirks and so on. By the way, we're going to have to stop at the store when we get to where we are going. Max is going to need diapers, food and such. I have ten cloth diapers but if we're going to be gone for a while I'll need more."

"We'll take care of you both, but I don't like waiting for a decision. You'll find out I don't have much patience. When I make a decision, it's a done deal, and you, my dear woman, are a done deal. We know and accept all the responsibilities that come with raising a child. We're not going to back away, Laura. We're in this for the long haul and maybe one day you'll let one of us adopt Max." Grant placed his finger on her lips. "You and Max will be our family." Grant leaned over and kissed her.

"We're here. Daniel, load the bags on the plane and have Badger Team Tango meet us at secured home three. I think that would be the best place for our woman and her son." Grant turned to him and winked as he opened the door and scanned the area.

"Where is this place? And where is Alex? I want to see her and make sure she is okay. You haven't even let me call her." Laura unhooked the car seat and handed it to him when he heard a loud scream coming from their right.

"Laura, is that you? Girl, you'd better get your ass over here and give me a hug!" A black woman with dreads down to her butt came running over and enfolded Laura in a hug.

Grant shook his head and greeted the other three members of their team while he spoke with air traffic control about getting clearance to head toward the mountains in Maine. Secured home three was their favorite getaway and their largest. With Laura's friend and two teams together again, they would need the space.

Talking into the phone, he smiled when Laura took the car seat showing off Max to Alex. His gaze traveled over Laura's best friend. She too was a full-figured woman, and with the way his friends and comrades kept staring at her, it looked as if she would be busy this week.

He grinned and nodded to Justin, Bo and Rafe. Wouldn't Alex be surprised to learn that all three men were sizing her up as their next conquest?

"Back off, Jolly Green Giant. I'm going to hold my godson and I don't need you crowding me," Alex snapped at Justin when he got a little too close.

"Soon, I'll show you how jolly I can be," Justin whispered in her ear but all of them caught it.

"See what you do to me, girl? I tell you, if I didn't love you, I'd be killing you right now." She rolled her eyes and scooped up a sleeping Max as he and Grant moved the women toward their private plane.

Laura yanked on his shirt and glared up at him. "Call off your goons. That was uncalled for."

Before Daniel could say anything, Grant reached

My Sugar Daddy

over and swatted her ass. "What is between your friend and them is none of our business. Now go get on the plane, both of you."

* * *

One minute Laura was glaring at Grant while walking toward the jet—the next all hell was breaking loose. Her ears were ringing and her arm and the left side of her body burned as something heavy shoved her to the ground with a grunt.

"Don't move. Daniel has Max and your friend is fine." Grant was whispering. Or was he yelling? She wasn't certain.

Lifting her head a fraction, Laura took in the scene around her. The private jet was now in flaming pieces. The two men who had been in front of her were now being seen by medics. Sirens blared in the distance as the ringing in her ears slowly tuned down.

"Are you hurt?" Daniel yelled, staring at her while covering her son's body with his. Laura heard his muffled cries, and tried to reach toward them, but a fierce shot of pain raced through the left side of her body, making her cry out.

The heavy weight on her back lifted and Grant rolled to her side. "Where?" Was all he said, but it was enough.

Very slowly, she rolled to her uninjured side, panting and moaning the whole time. She looked down to her side and everything started to spin. Her clothes were almost melded to her skin; a small piece of the plane was sticking out of her side.

"Son of a bitch. Gary, we need you here. Seth,

bring the Hummer and park it in front of us. Justin, Bo, you get Alex back into the car. Daniel, put Max in the Hummer, but have Seth check him out first. He's worked on infants before."

All of Grant's words blurred together as people ran around doing what he ordered.

"No hospitals. I have no insurance, plus it's not as bad as it looks." Laura tried to peel the shirt away from her skin but someone reached out and held onto her hand.

"No, let me check it first. Can you roll onto your back for me so I can get a better look?" The tattoo-faced man was speaking and she nodded in acceptance.

Sucking in her breath, Laura rolled to her back and stared up at the man. His piercing green eyes reminded her of the pictures of her father. "You have amazing eyes. They remind me of my father's." Laura blurted it out before she could even stop herself. "Sorry."

He smiled. "Thank you. Now, let's see how bad off you are." The giant man's hands were gentle on her flesh but the slightest touch hurt like hell.

"You have a few burns. Nothing life-threatening, but you have several small pieces of metal in your side I need to remove. I can give you a sedative and it will help with the pain. We need to clean your skin so infection doesn't set in."

He reached over to the small black bag he'd brought over and pulled out a needle and a small bottle.

"No! I don't want any shots. Just do it," Laura ordered. There was no way she was going to be drugged up when her son needed her.

My Sugar Daddy

The car pulled in front of them. She watched Daniel put Max and his car seat into the Hummer. She tried to ignore the pain as Seth slowly peeled her shirt away and started to pick out the pieces of metal.

Many of them were small, but when Seth looked up at Laura she knew he'd come to the larger piece. "Do it."

She clenched her fingers, only to have Grant at her side twining his hand with hers. "You should have taken the shot, but I understand why you didn't. Hopefully soon you'll learn to trust us." He leaned down and kissed her lips softly distracting her as Seth yanked the piece out of her skin.

"Shit, that hurt!" Laura gasped and squeezed Grant's hand.

"It's out. Hold still while I put these butterfly bandages on. I'll have a tube of antibiotic cream for you later when we settle down. Wear dresses if you can. That way nothing will rub or stick to your skin. Grant, do you have one of your shirts we can slip on her?"

For the next half hour, Gary, Daniel and Grant worked on cleaning her cuts and abrasions. Finally, they were satisfied they'd gotten each injury. Grant helped her into one of his shirts when they were finished. Their men surrounding her making sure no one else saw what they were doing.

If she weren't in such pain, Laura knew she would have been embarrassed. Cradling her in his arms, Grant got into the Hummer. Daniel and Seth followed, as did Gary.

"Head to Akron. My father has another plane arriving there in the next hour," Daniel ordered Seth as he pulled the Hummer into traffic.

Leaning over Grant's arm, Laura pulled Max's blanket up over his small body and sighed. "Thank you, Daniel, for saving him."

"I'm just sorry you got hurt. We never thought they would target you." Daniel turned in his seat and leaned back to kiss the top of his head. "Sleep. We'll wake you up when we get to the airport."

Resting her head on Grant's shoulder, Laura closed her eyes while her hand remained on Max's car seat. Her life was in shambles and there wasn't a damn thing she could do about it. Not only had she endangered her life but also Max's and Alex's.

Today was right up there with her mom dying as the worst-possible day in her life.

Chapter Seven

Stepping onto the plane, Grant carried a sleeping Laura. It hadn't taken her long to fall fast asleep, and she wasn't the only one. He smiled as Rafe carried a passed-out Alex.

"Jed and Torch are on their way. They spoke with the captain and explained everything to him. The local press is being told an older jet exploded while fueling." Daniel placed the baby carrier on the seat in front of them strapping it down.

His brother sat down next to him and carefully placed Laura's feet into his lap. "I don't want her at the condo. I want her at our house." Daniel took Laura's shoes off and started to rub her feet. "When she went flying backward...I don't know how or why, but I can't let her go."

The sound of a bird screaming drew his attention and Daniel looked out the window, staring in disbelief. He swore it was the same bird from earlier sitting on the wing of the plane and staring at their window. "Do you see what I do?"

"It's Momma. She's watching over us," Laura mumbled, peeking around him to stare out the window. "Thanks for taking such good care of Max for me." She took his hand in his and kissed it.

"You should be resting. I suppose you heard what I said?" Daniel watched as she leaned back into Grant's arms, wincing once, and nodded.

"We agreed to take this time to see what happens between us, but Daniel, I do feel something or I wouldn't be sitting here with you right now. I wouldn't have trusted you with my son while I slept. All I can tell you is I have to take it slow. What you two are asking for is out of the norm, and I've had nothing but bad luck when it comes to men." She kissed Grant's chest.

"We'll wait. We have plenty of time. I'm afraid we might be awhile at the secured location." Daniel glanced at his brother who nodded.

His brother stood and placed Laura into his lap. "I have a few things to check on and I want to make sure we have everything we'll need for Max. I had Seth check in your bag and found the formula for Max but is he eating anything else? What size diapers does he need? Are you allergic to any foods?"

Laura smiled. "Max will need cereal and baby food. There is a box in the bag. Also, he has a prescription for these drops, which I'll need filled again in a few weeks. He's already into the large diapers—he is into a three or four. He's about 22 pounds so whatever brand you go for, just have them check the size. I'm allergic to certain fruits— apples, peaches, plums. I drink two-percent milk because I'm lactose-intolerant even though I should drink the almond stuff, but can't afford it. Other than that, I'm fine. Oh, and make sure there is plenty of dark-roast coffee, please."

"Like your coffee, do you?" Grant said and

My Sugar Daddy

smiled. "Okay, got it, and I'll have them fill the prescription right away. Anything else?"

Her face turned a rosy color and she fiddled with his shirt. "Well, if we're going to, umm, you know, we'll need some kind of protection. I had to have my IUD taken out."

"Don't worry about that. We'll take care of you, and we'll most definitely be doing a lot of that," Daniel teased her, brushing his fingers across her hardened nipple. "But first you are to rest and heal. Let us take care of you, Laura."

She didn't say anything, but turned her head to stare at Alex, who was watching their every move from Rafe's arms. Her gaze landed on him, then on Grant. "You hurt my friend and I swear I'll find you and rip your balls off. She's been through too much with her mom dying, that dickhead using her, the threatening letters and her tires being slashed."

"Alex, enough! It's in the past. We have to let it go." Laura tried to sit up and her face tightened as she gripped his arm tight to lift herself.

"You're going to rip those stitches! Lie back down," Daniel ordered but she ignored him as she scooted off his lap and into the seat Grant had been sitting in.

"I want to talk to Alex for a little while. You two go do your business and let us girls talk. I'll rest later, I promise." She patted his leg and smiled at him. "But I think both of us could use a nice stiff drink."

Laura laughed as Alex slapped Rafe's hands when he tried to keep her from getting up. "Let go you big oaf! I want to talk to my girl." She continued slapping at Rafe's hand, but kept laughing as he nipped at her neck.

"Fine, but you will put your feet up and rest. You also need to eat something before you have a drink. You didn't eat anything earlier," Rafe ordered, placing her across from Laura.

"I'll have the flight attendant make you both some sandwiches and some coffee. We'll save the drinks for later when we get settled into the house." Daniel leaned down and placed a kiss on her cheek. "Cream, no sugar, right?"

Looking up at him, she smiled. "Yep, thank you. I am a bit hungry."

"I meant what I said, Laura. We are here to take care of you. Grant and I will always be there for you." Daniel stood and made his way to the galley. Rounding the corner into the kitchen he stopped, shocked to see his mother and sister there making sandwiches and coffee.

"What the hell are you two doing here? Does Dad know?" Daniel growled. His mother turned sharply, pointing her finger at him.

"Don't you get all snippy with me, and yes, your father is here too. Do you really think we wouldn't be after we heard about the other plane? Plus, it gives me time to meet this woman you two are so protective of." She grabbed a tray of sandwiches while his sister Tracy grabbed the coffee and cups.

"Move out of the way. I'm sure those two girls are famished after all they went through." His mother bumped into his hip and pushed him out of the way.

"Mom..." He turned to watch his mother and sister make their way up the aisle toward Laura.

"Don't worry, your mother knows what she is doing. Now come. Grant is waiting for us below." His

My Sugar Daddy

father slapped him on his back. "The rest of the family will meet us at the house in Maine. They're also readying a room for the child."

He sighed and nodded as he followed his father down the stairs where Grant and about 15 of their men were seated around the table. At first glance, he knew his brother was no happier than he was about having their family here. It meant worrying not only about Laura, Max and Alex, but now their family.

"Team three needs to be called in and the bunker house needs to be readied." Grant ordered.

He flipped his phone open before he even sat down. Now was the time to prepare for full-scale battle.

* * *

Furious was the only thing she could think of to describe how she felt right now. Not only had she and her friend been exposed to danger, but now she had to deal with his mom and sister?

"Thank you for the food and coffee. You two really didn't have to do this. Neither Daniel or Grant mentioned you were here." She looked to Alex, who looked as if she was ready to kill someone.

"They didn't know, and of course we'd come. Our sons' private plane was bombed. We are a very close family and when one of us is under attack, we all are. Now, please, tell me about yourself. Are your parents from Ohio?" Daniel and Grant's mother Nadine quizzed Laura.

Her best friend leaned over and squeezed her hand. "Laura's mother died a year ago today from cancer, and she never knew her father." Alex's gaze never left hers as she smiled. "I suppose she left you a sign too?"

She laughed so hard her side hurt. "You do know my mom. Yes, as a matter of fact, she visited both Grant and Daniel earlier. Mom has already approved them." Laura looked out the window, hoping to see the red-tail hawk, but it was gone.

"My mom had a way with animals and plants. She was very in tune with everything around her, so when we found out she had cancer—well, it was a big surprise." Laura looked at Nadine, who crouched next to her.

"I'm so sorry. Your mother was a witch or pagan? Is that what they are called now?" She looked up at her daughter Tracy who nodded.

"One of my brothers practices himself so we have some experience with this. I am truly sorry about your mother though. It seems as if the big C has encroached in everyone's life at least once. My mom lost her grandmother to breast cancer when I was six." She nodded to the seat on the other side of Max's car seat. "May I?"

"Please." Laura patted the seat next to her for Nadine to sit. "My mom didn't suffer long. By the time we found out she had it, it had already spread throughout her body. She lived about two months longer, but she didn't let a minute go by without doing all she could."

"I don't mean to change the subject, but where is the father of your son?" Nadine asked, peeking into the car seat and smiling down at Max.

"I don't mind. I appreciate your forwardness.

My Sugar Daddy

Max's father doesn't want anything to do with him. He's signed over total custody and rights to me. Let's just say his father was a total ass and leave it at that." She took a bit of the sandwich and moaned. "This is fantastic. What is it?"

Nadine smiled and patted her leg. "It's like a Reuben, but with a twist. It has everything a Reuben does, but I add goat cheese to it."

"Wow." Alex took another bite and moaned. "Why do I have a feeling we're going to gain 600 pounds being around this family?" She stuffed another bite into her mouth.

Tracy laughed and patted her round stomach.

"Believe me, I know. I've been working out for the past three months trying to get rid of this gut, but every time I turn around, Mom is cooking up something or trying something new. It doesn't help that she runs one of the best catering gigs in New York."

Her friend laughed and almost choked on the food in her mouth. "I'm sorry, but this is too good. You couldn't ask for a better family, Laura, I mean really—a catering business and a wizard to boot? What about Grant and Daniel? Can they do anything different?" Alex shook her head and took another bite of her sandwich.

"Alex!" She kicked her friend's leg. "Sorry. Alex gets ahead of herself."

"What? You have both men drooling all over you. Do you really believe they're going to let you go? Not going to happen, sister. I've seen those looks on their faces when they watch you."

Her face heated and she turned to their mother, who was smiling. "She's right. I saw the way both of my sons were, and not to worry. I've known my sons share their women for a while, but, then again, so does half of our family. It's the first time in a while Grant has been interested in anything other than his last call of duty. I can almost see the old Grant and the sparkle in his eyes he had before he left. You brought him out of his shell, and for that I will always thank you. Now, tell me, do you like to cook?"

"Mom, she's supposed to be resting, not answering all your questions," Grant said, leaning down and picking her up, almost spilling her coffee.

"Grant, I'm fine, and your mom's food well makes up for the questions. If you didn't want her talking to me, then you should have stayed. You both took off fast enough." She slapped his arm and turned back to his mom as soon as he settled in the seat with her on his lap.

"Yes, I love to cook. Mom and I used to cook up a storm. We used to grow all our own herbs and stuff too. I miss that." She sipped her coffee.

"You have to make some more lavender soap and lotion. I'm almost out and I love that stuff." Alex took a sip of her coffee. "But then again, I never did try your cranberry soap."

"What? You make all these?" Nadine asked as she and Tracy both stood and moved out into the aisle. Daniel and some other man came toward them.

"It's been awhile. The last bunch Mom and I made right before she died, but yes, we used to make our own shampoo, soap and lotion. Where is my bag?"

She looked around for it as Daniel handed it to her. She dug down in the bottom and pulled out one of the small bottles of lotion. "Here, try this. I have three

My Sugar Daddy

of them with me." Laura placed the bag onto the floor as Daniel sat down next to them.

"Laura, this is my father, Richard." Grant nodded to the man who swept his arm around Nadine, who opened the small bottle and smelled.

"It's a pleasure to meet you. I just wish it were under better terms," Laura said and placed her hand in his father's.

He leaned down and kissed her knuckles. "I can see why my sons are quite taken with you. You are beautiful."

Nadine rolled her eyes and elbowed him out of the way. "Cool it, Casanova. Laura, this stuff is amazing. We will be talking later, young lady, and you two?" She gestured to Grant and Daniel. "Don't mess this up. She's a keeper." At that, their dad shuffled her down the plane to sit three seats behind them.

"Sorry. We had no idea they would fly up here with the plane." Grant kissed the side of her neck and placed her in the seat between him and Daniel. "We're about to take off. Buckle up." He reached over and pulled the strap across his lap but stopped before he latched the seatbelt.

"This isn't going to rub any sore spots, is it?" He tried to lift the shirt she wore but Laura held it down.

"No, they are up closer to my breast. And stop. You don't need me to flash everyone."

She nodded to Rafe, who had just picked up her squawking friend Alex.

"I don't care who sees. Your health is more important than a free shot. Now move your hands, Laura, and let me check," Grant demanded, his gaze holding hers.

"Fine." She put her hands at her side as he lifted the shirt, checking to make sure the seatbelt didn't rub against her wounds. Satisfied, Grant lowered the top, covering her back up before buckling the belt.

"I told you," she mumbled and tried to pull the shirt down further.

Taking two of his fingers, Grant lifted her chin 'til she stared into his gaze. "When it comes to your health or safety, nothing matters more. If it makes you uncomfortable I'm sorry, but I will not risk hurting you. We've put you in enough danger, and we'll be making it up to you for a long time to come." Leaning down, he covered her lips with his.

He traced his tongue along the seam of her lips, then slid inside and caressed her tongue in a slow seduction. She moaned and leaned into the kiss wanting more, but he broke the kiss.

"Umm, what were we talking about?" She grinned.

"I wanted to talk to you about your apartment. I have a team there packing it up. I don't know how long we'll be here and I want you to be comfortable with your own things." Grant took her coffee from her before she dropped it.

"You moved my whole apartment?" She squeaked a little, but all of a sudden things were moving just too fast.

Chapter Eight

Two hours on the plane and it was the quietest he'd seen Laura. Only talking when she needed to and seeing to her son's needs. Ever since his brother had mentioned Laura's belongings were being packed up, she hadn't said much.

Even when Grant told her they were getting ready to land, she just nodded. Daniel watched as she changed Max, getting him ready to leave the plane. It was a little cooler at Eagle Lake but it was well worth it.

She stood, looked down at her attire and frowned.

"I have this for you. It should cover all of you." Daniel held up a long coat and she smiled at him.

"Thank you. I need to apologize to your brother. I over-reacted earlier. It just feels as if I don't belong anywhere. At least with my apartment, it was my own. I don't know where I stand with you two and it's a little scary." She looked down at her feet and laughed. "Umm, do you by any chance have boots?"

Looking down, he laughed. "Not to worry. I'll carry you to the car. Tomorrow we'll go into town and get anything else we need." He kissed the top of her head. "And sweetie, we're not going anywhere. Who knows, maybe we'll stay out here for a while. We can work anywhere." He scooped her up as Seth grabbed Max's carrier.

Everyone had departed the plane and she watched for Grant. Daniel had been right—there was a chill in the air. "Seth, will you make sure that blanket is tight around Max? It's a little colder than I realized." She smiled back at him and noticed Grant taking up the rear. He never once looked toward her.

"Daniel, are you sure Grant's not mad at me?" Daniel bent down and she slid into the car with him climbing in right next to her.

"Yes, I'm sure. He has to meet our supervisor, so he'll be taking another car and meeting us at the house." He kissed the top of her head and slid his arm around her while she hooked her son into the seat.

Curling up next to Daniel, Laura took in the breathtaking scene. From what Daniel had told her, they had 60 miles yet to go. All along the road he pointed things out, telling her stories about his previous family visits.

Even though the house was theirs, it was kept in a trust's name, which kept anyone from knowing who owned the property. It was their personal getaway and one of the top safe houses used by their team, he told her.

After stopping for a few items, Seth drove the car around the grand circular drive; Laura sat there stunned. When he had told her they would be staying at the small house, she thought it would be a two or three-bedroom house—not a six-bedroom log mansion.

"You call this small?" she asked, getting out, slowly spinning around, taking in all she could. Laura didn't even care if her feet were a little cold.

My Sugar Daddy

About 300 yards away to the left stood the larger dwelling, and Seth hadn't been kidding. Three stories, six wings from what he told her. The estate itself was over 200 acres. According to Daniel, his twin cousins managed the ranch when no one was around. They raised draft horses, buffalo and pigs on the property.

"If we stay for the summer, there is a large place over by the smaller barn where you could plant anything you like." Daniel said, once more carefully picking her up and walking into the house. "Tomorrow we'll get you and Alex some boots and winter clothes, since your things won't be here for a few days."

Setting her down in the family room, Laura once more twirled around and smiled. "Wow!" She and Alex spoke at the same time as Rafe brought her in.

"Look at this place. My apartment could fit in this room alone." Alex ran her hand along the stone fireplace. "They have three sofas. Can you believe that?"

Laura took the car seat from Seth and sat on one of the couches. "Come here, little guy. I bet you're sick of that seat, aren't you?"

She picked up a smiling Max, who was babbling up a storm as he took in the place. "Daniel, would you spread the blanket on the floor? We'll let him roll around for a few minutes."

"Let's put it on this rug." Daniel picked up a coffee table and moved it out of the way before spreading out the blanket. "This way if he rolls over on the hard floor, he won't hurt his head." He took Max out of her arms and placed him in the middle of the blanket while she tossed his toys around the blanket.

"Rafe, why don't you take Alex downstairs and show her where she'll be staying?" As they left, Daniel sat down on one of the couches and pulled Laura in between his legs. "Alone at last. Open the shirt, Laura. I want to see the extent of your injuries and then I'm going to show you to our room, where I want you to take a nice hot bath. I'll watch Max for you."

She cocked her head to the side and studied him as she opened the large dress shirt. Even sitting, he was a big man with broad shoulders. He was muscular but not overly so. He had a tattoo running down the side of his neck and under his T-shirt. Just the way he carried himself impressed her.

As he opened her shirt, he sat up and traced lightly over every scratch and cut. "I know we haven't known each other long, but when that plane blew… We're lucky we weren't closer." He leaned in and kissed each cut, each scratch. "Even cut up, you are gorgeous." He slid his hands up her stomach and cupped her breasts, lifting them to his mouth.

"So big. Even your nipples are large. I need a taste." She held onto his shoulders. He sucked her right nipple into his mouth, while his other hand tweaked and rolled her other nipple.

"Daniel…you have to stop. Anyone could walk in." Laura tried to step back, but he held her tight.

One little nip and he lifted his head to look up at her. "We are in my house and all our men know the rules. They knock before coming in." He released her and stood but not before giving her butt a little tap.

"Hey." She laughed and jumped away from him.

Ignoring her yelp, he reached down and picked up Max, moving to the hallway. "Come on. Your bags and the things we ordered for you should be in the room."

Following behind him, Laura held the shirt closed as they moved up the winding staircase and down the hall.

"The first two rooms are guest rooms and a bath for them. This room here is where I thought we could set up a nursery." He opened the door and she gasped.

A crib with bumper pads was set up in the middle of the room, and there were blankets, diapers, lotion—everything she would need. The walls were a pale blue and there was even a brand-new baby monitor.

"You've done too much, Daniel. This stuff is expensive." She teared up when she saw the bouncy thing she had wanted to buy for Max but hadn't been able to afford.

His arm came around her and he squeezed. "Laura, nothing is too much for you two. Our room is connected, so it will be easy to get up in the night to check on him." He opened the door and she was surprised again.

The bed was the largest she'd ever seen and the room featured a balcony with a hot tub on it off to one side. A fireplace beckoned from one corner and two walk-in closets had plenty of room to stow her clothes. But what had her jaw dropping was the small alcove.

On one wall was an assortment of paddles, canes and whips, while on the other sat dildos, butt plugs, oils and other different toys she didn't even recognize. On the far wall was something she knew had to be a St. Andrew's Cross. But the thing that had her stomach flipping was the doctor-like table with stirrups in the middle of the room.

"Like that table, do you? The walls in this alcove have been insulated. No sounds will be heard in Max's room." He gently coaxed her out of the room and pushed a button on his key ring. "Both Grant and I have keys to this room, but no one else does. We've never brought anyone to this room. Everything is brand new, as is the bedroom. We've been waiting a very long time for you, Laura." She watched as a panel slid out and shut off the alcove.

It was as if the niche wasn't even there by the time the wall was in place. "It's also a safe room. There is a small staircase hidden in the floor, which we'll show you tomorrow. Go on now. The bath is through that door there and everything should be set out for you." He patted her butt and guided her toward the one door she hadn't peeked into yet.

"When you're done, come downstairs. The folks are bringing out the grills; we're cooking outside tonight."

He turned to leave but she placed her hand on his back. "Daniel?"

Turning, he stared at her. "I want to thank you for everything you've done. You didn't have to do this. You and your brother make me feel special. I've never had that before, even with the asshole." She smiled up at him.

"We will always put your needs before ours, little one. You have a bright soul— how can we not want you in our lives? We've only just begun, baby. Now take your bath." He leaned down and although he barely touched her lips with his, her insides heated.

The door closed behind her and Laura looked around the space. On the counter lay a green dress with a small note. "You will need no undergarments here."

She laughed and lightly touched the dress, realizing it was silk. "Beautiful."

My Sugar Daddy

After a half hour of soaking in the tub, Laura felt like a new person. Her bath salts had been placed in the bathroom. She had chosen honeysuckle, one of her favorites. The dress was smooth on her skin and she loved how it curved to her body.

The door behind her cracked open. In the mirror, she watched Grant step into the bathroom behind her. He gently took the brush out of her hand and started to brush her hair. "I wanted to apologize to you for my reaction earlier. I know you are only helping me but at the time…" She sighed and looked down. "It seemed as if everything came at me at once. I felt lost, as if I had nothing. With the apartment…it was my own, so no one could throw me out."

He wrapped his arms around her and kissed the side of her neck. "There is no reason to apologize. We know this is happening fast. I just wish we didn't have this threat hanging over our heads." He turned her around and cupped her face. "I have good news though. We've recovered your mother's body. For now, we are going to bury her in a private cemetery here in Maine, where no one can get at her. Is that okay with you?"

She slowly inched her arms around his neck and reached up to kiss his chin. "Thank you. That would be fine. As long as I know she is safe."

* * *

Daniel met them at the stairs. Laura was stunning in the dress Grant had picked for her. Daniel was grateful his other brothers had arrived before them and gotten the house ready—he'd have to thank them later.

"Are you ready?" Daniel asked. "I took one of the bottles you had ready for Max and fed him. I even gave him a bath and changed his clothes, so he's all ready for bed." He handed Max to her and she smiled.

"Thank you. You are the first to ever help me with him. I don't know how you arranged everything in his room and ours, but it is impressive." Her stomach growled and Grant laughed.

"Come on. I have a nice long sweater to go with the dress. The flats fit, I see." Both men escorted her toward the back door, where Grant held out a dark green sweater for her.

"Yes, they are a perfect fit. Grant, are those two men okay? You know the ones who were in front of us? I felt so bad leaving them there without making sure they were going to make it."

Walking toward their folks' house, Grant informed her of the condition of their men. Both would be arriving here in a few days as their wounds not life threatening. He glanced to the left to see Alex coming down the sidewalk with Rafe, Justin and Bo.

She too wore a dress, but this was a bright-red one that hugged her curves and set off her dusky skin. "Do I take it the three of them are interested in my friend?" Laura nudged him and whispered to him.

He laughed and nodded. "Yes, and they'll take great care of her, I promise. If they don't, I'll personally kill the three of them."

Grabbing hold of his T-shirt, Laura yanked on it 'til he lowered his head where she kissed him. "Thank you. She's all I have left. When Mom died, she was the only one there for me."

They walked around the corner and she stopped.

My Sugar Daddy

"Damn, how many men do you have?" Laura asked, biting her lower lip.

"They are all here to protect you and our family. I have five teams of 20 of the finest former Marine, Air Force, Navy and Army operatives here under my command. When there is a threat, we pull together. We are the only group of our kind in the world. It's one of the reasons why we're always on call. We have two other teams spread out, searching for those who would harm us. My men are only called in as a last resort, but when one of their own is threatened, they all come." Grant stared out at the men who crowded around the grills, talking.

"We have this whole place surrounded with alarms and men," Grant said. "If anyone steps onto this land, we will know."

Hearing the sadness in Grant's voice, Laura rubbed her head on his arm. "I've been told I'm a great listener if you ever want to talk."

Grant looked at Daniel, then down at Laura. "I'm fine, but thank you. Maybe one day I'll be able to open up, but I can't now. It's still too raw. Having you here with us helps more than you know." Grant kissed her forehead. "Come, Mom is waiting for us."

As they walked up to the grill, Nadine and Tracy pulled Alex and Laura into the house, talking up a storm. Daniel and Grant waited to hear what the general had to say.

The general reported to the president about their orders.

"The general has given me the green light and he has ordered Samuel's teams to be ready if we need them. Dad has closed the offices for the next two weeks and the rest of the family will be here tomorrow." Grant took a swig of his beer, observing everything around them.

"What aren't you telling us?" Seth asked as Daniel leaned against one of the large oak trees. Justin, Rafe, Bo, Seth and Zenith stood around them while others all turned toward him, waiting for the other shoe to drop.

"Get Alex and Laura out here. They should hear this too." Grant ran his hand through his hair.

"We're here. What's wrong?" Laura pushed through the men with Alex to stand in front of them.

"I'm sorry. My men were in the process of packing up the rest of your belongings, Laura, when they were attacked. We have one small truckload coming but the rest we lost along with the building. Thirteen civilians were killed and the building was leveled. Alex, your house is gone. By the time we got there, it was burning to the ground. We couldn't save anything."

"Those motherfuckers!" Alex yelled as she and Laura held onto each other.

"How many of your men were hurt?" Laura asked. "Most of our things can be replaced, but men can't."

A strong surge of pride went through Grant, and Daniel leaned down and kissed her cheek. "A few were hurt, but they will survive. Thank you for your concern." Grant straightened up and scanned the men moving in around them.

"Those of you who have families, call them. We have enough room for them here. The plane is ready to pick them up. We'll make this our home base because it looks as if we are going to be here a while. Zenith, I want you to take ten men and go into town tomorrow.

My Sugar Daddy

The general and I have ordered ten mobile homes to be delivered. We'll set them up on the east pasture there and hook them up to electricity. That pasture is surrounded on three sides by the mountains, so it's well protected. If we need more homes we'll call and order them. This way, those who do have families will have something private. For the rest of you, there are the bunkers for you to use."

Reaching out, Daniel wrapped his arm around Laura's waist. Her body shook as she rested her head on his chest. "How can I help? I want to do my part—these people need to be stopped. I didn't know anyone in my apartment building, but they didn't deserve this."

He heard the sadness in her voice, but she was seemingly trying to be strong for them. "We're going to have over 100 men here, and some families. Why don't you, Mom and Alex put together lists of things we'll need for food and such? Mom knows how to cook for large groups of people, but she'll need help."

"I've already called the next farm over," Nadine said, stepping forward. "They raise fine-grade beef and we've gotten many cows from them. I've told them we're going to need at least ten for now, slaughtered and cut up. Your father has the walk-in freezers in the basement where we can store the meat for now, but maybe we can build a special kitchen and mess hall for everyone in the new barn. It's never been used but it's big enough, and the men could maybe put some kind of rec center down there for themselves. We're lucky we're going into summer—Laura and I can plant plenty of food. We also have the bison too." Nadine turned and glanced at Richard.

"That small shed would make a great chicken

coop. We could have our own fresh eggs to save us from going into town. Maybe some turkeys too, but we're still going to draw attention with this many men here." Laura looked to Grant and he nodded.

"I'm sure they are already aware we are here. We are lucky our town is small. I've been ordered to place the town on notice. We have men surrounding it as we speak. The mayor and the sheriff have been notified and they will be here shortly to discuss things. One good thing about this town is there is only one way into it and it's being watched as we speak. It will be a lot easier to protect against threats." He sighed and looked at his men.

"The president has designated the town and the surrounding area as our own personal base. I'll be going into town with Daniel to speak with the town people tomorrow. They all will have a choice—we're offering to buy their land or they can stay. Either way we will protect everyone who stays."

"I'd like to go into town with you. Maybe having us around will help ease the other women. We can help too." Laura turned in his arms to face Grant.

Grant shook his head. "I don't want you off this property, Laura. You've been through enough and I won't risk your life. Think of your son."

She stiffened in Daniel's arms. "I want to help and I'm good at organizing things. Alex can watch Max for me while we're gone. Nadine, let's go make a list while the food cooks. Alex, you coming?" She stepped out of Daniel's arms only to be yanked into Grant's arms.

"I mean it, Laura, you're not going, and that is final." Grant shook her a little.

My Sugar Daddy

"Let me go, *now*. This is not over. We will discuss this tonight, not in front of your men." She latched onto Alex's hand, getting away from Daniel and Grant before either could do anything.

Their mom laughed and followed Laura and Alex into the house. His father shook his head, smiling. "She's a keeper, that one. Has the strength to stand up to the both of you. Now tell me, how dangerous are we talking here." His father was all business. Any threat to his family and his father would let nothing stand in his way.

"They're just not hitting our family. It seems that they are hitting at strategic places in the U.S. Places where Hager believed our teams were stationed. Hager not only has had time to rebuild his army, but it looks as if he's joined forces with a number of operatives from Europe. The president has been informed and, at present, the public thinks terrorists are to blame. A total of six additional targets have been hit—two in New York, two in two in Texas and two in California, along with the attacks in Ohio. Death toll so far is 63 and rising. I'm afraid we won't be going back to New York any time soon. We've been told to stay put for the summer, at least until things settle down. For right now the president wants us hidden until we have the largest target."

"Do we have locations on any of them?" Daniel asked, moving away from the tree.

"Yes, we have two of Hager's headquarters under surveillance now. Until I get word, we are just to watch. These are small units. I want the big one and I'm hoping they will lead us to it. That's when we make our move, not before." Grant looked up at the house, then back at Daniel. "We have to stay together on this, Daniel. I don't want her out there."

He nodded. "I'm with you. If it means so much to her, we can have the women meet here on some days, as long as they have passed security clearance."

His brother nodded. "Good. It's settled." Grant looked toward the house. Both knew Laura and their family were all that mattered.

Chapter Nine

Laura stood at the sliding glass door burping Max as she watched more Hummers pulling in and men getting out carrying duffle bags. In just two hours, the area swarmed with military men.

One of the large mobile homes had arrived early and, using it as their command post, Grant and Daniel began setting up equipment while they ate.

"Why do I feel as if we are in the Twilight Zone?" Alex asked, turning and shaking her head. "Even on the news they aren't saying much about the bombings." She pulled out a chair at the table and sat next to Nadine and her daughter.

"I have to say, I've never seen it this bad, but then when my son formed this special team, the Badgers or whatever they call themselves, I knew then things would change." Nadine tapped the pen on the table. "So, do we need anything else for the garden?"

Laura shook her head. "No, you have everything we'll need. I noticed you have grape vines and a strawberry patch. We'll be able to make our own jelly and soaps too. I've added the few things we'll need for that. We might want to also think about wintertime. If we're going to be stuck here, we should stock up on coats, boots and such for everyone."

"That has been taken care of. Supplies have already started to arrive. We have enough MRE's to last for two years stored in the cellar under the barn and a truckload of coats, boats and fatigues arrived less than a half hour ago." Daniel said, coming in and kissing her head. "It's getting late and everyone is settling down. Come on, let's go home. Mom, I'll come by in the morning for that list. Alex, Rafe is waiting for you." He scooped up Max's carrier and urged Laura outside to the path toward her new temporary home.

Behind them, Rafe and Alex followed, but no one said anything. Laura kissed Alex on the cheek and went up the stairs once inside. Daniel stood at the bottom of the stairs and spoke to Rafe but Laura ignored them, preparing for the battle to come.

Oh, she knew Grant wouldn't allow her to go, but she would say her piece. She knew they both wanted to protect her and Max, but acting like a caveman in front of everyone would have to go.

Of course, she would rely on Grant and Daniel for protection. She wasn't stupid. "They're just going to have to back off with the badass routine," she assured Max. "You've been so good today. Mommy loves you, sweetie. Things will settle soon, I promise." She changed Max and slipped on one of the new sleepers they had gotten for him.

"Sleep well, little guy." Laura covered him with the blanket and grabbed the handheld monitor, turning it on before she walked into the bedroom and closed the door behind her.

She jumped when warm arms surrounded her from behind, careful of her side. "Badass, ha." Grant

My Sugar Daddy

nipped her ear and turned her to face him. His shirt was off and he was barefoot.

"Yes." She lifted her head and ducked under his arm, getting away from him. She noticed the little alcove was now open, but her nervousness would not deter her from confronting them.

"Take off the dress, Laura, and come to me," Grant ordered.

"No! We will talk before we go any further." Laura stood her ground as Daniel came into the room and stripped off his shirt. Daniel looked from her to Grant.

"Trouble already?" Daniel asked. Grant frowned.

"There is no trouble," Laura said. "I want to speak to both of you. I know I was wrong to ask to go with you tomorrow." She sighed and sat on the bed. "I shouldn't have confronted you in front of your men, and I'm sorry, but you were wrong too." She looked up as both men came to stand beside her.

"I want to be treated as a partner. I'm not stupid, and I know you two will take care of us, but I would like some consideration, because you embarrassed me too. I know I'm right about the women of this town. If they feel threatened, their men will also. I just thought a woman's presence might help, but you completely dismissed me without even considering what I said. All I'm asking is that you listen to me." Laura looked up at Grant.

He held out his hand and she placed her smaller one into his as he tugged her into his arms. "You're right and I'm sorry, but I still don't want you going with us. Until the town is secure, I need you to stay here. When the town is secure, we'll see. Daniel did have an idea." Grant kissed a path down to her neck and bit her shoulder before yanking her dress up and over her head.

"I thought we could set up a type of web-com you could speak from home but still be there," Daniel said, squeezing her ass. "And if the women still had questions they could email them to you. My brother is a computer geek. He'll set it all up and make sure it's secure. Now go get on the table, Laura."

Both men stepped away from her and Laura would have fallen back onto the bed if Grant hadn't studied her before releasing her. She eyed the exam table and slowly moved to it, only glancing back once at both Grant and Daniel.

"I'm scared," she admitted. "I haven't done any of this stuff." Her voice was a whisper, but they heard her and were next to her in a second.

"We will never hurt you. Do you believe that?" Grant helped her onto the stool near the table so she wouldn't have to jump up.

Turning to scoot on the table, she nodded and took a deep breath. "Yes, I trust you."

"Lie back and put your feet in the stirrups, sweetheart. We need to stretch you, so both of us can take you." Daniel assisted her in putting her feet up and strapping them to the table. "Have you ever had anyone make love to that fine ass of yours?" he said sliding his fingers down her wet pussy lips to her nether hole, tapping it.

Taking her hands, Grant lifted them and tied a silk scarf around them, attaching it to the table. "It is easy to get out of if you have to but I want you to try to stay put." He leaned down and kissed each of her

My Sugar Daddy

cheeks. "Put some of that cream Seth gave us on her sores first."

As they moved to her left side, both men examined her wounds. "Do they hurt?" Grant's worried expression met hers and she smiled. "Just when I move wrong. They itch more than anything." Grant nodded, turning toward a shelf.

"Tonight, we will come together as one. To do this, we must stretch you, but with your injuries I want you to really try not to move. Let us take care of you and your pleasure." Daniel bent his head and sucked her nipple into his mouth.

"Daniel!" She arched up and flinched. At once his mouth was gone and he frowned down at her. "This isn't going to work."

Walking to her other side, Daniel lifted her breast and nodded. He reached for the strap and tightened it around her upper body, away from the stitches. "This will keep you still. I don't want you hurting yourself."

Once more Daniel lowered his head and sucked her nipple into his mouth. He smiled around her nipple as she tried to lift up but couldn't. A small moan escaped her. "So sensitive—and look at how big your nipples get. Let's try some clamps, shall we?" He opened a pair of nipple clamps. Daniel knew she wasn't ready for the alligator clamps because of her inexperience. These feather clamps would work perfectly for her.

Stepping between Laura's legs, Grant coated his fingers with lube and prepared to stretch her slowly. Tonight would be about her, showing her she was meant to be with them. Daniel and Grant had watched her all evening and were pleased by the way she pitched in and helped those around her. Never once did she complain, even though she'd had one seriously bad day.

Yes. Laura was their woman, and they were not about to let her go—ever.

As Daniel screwed the clamp into place, Laura whimpered and tossed her head to the side. "Easy, baby," Grant murmured. "These are beginner clamps. Now I'm going to stretch you with my fingers. Another time we'll use the butt plugs too, but tonight you're tired."

Soon they would start her training, but tonight they just wanted her to get used to the table and her surroundings. As soon as Grant opened her up, they would move her to the bed, claiming her as theirs.

During the course of the day, both Daniel and Grant had noticed how self-conscious Laura was of her stomach. She was always making sure her tummy never showed and that her shirt was pulled down to cover it.

Kissing his way down her belly, Daniel gently squeezed the roll of love she had. "So freaking beautiful. Every inch of you is like silk. I can reach for you and not be afraid I'll break you." He kissed and licked her stomach.

"Never be ashamed of your body. It's perfect just the way it is." Grant said, tonguing her mound.

"My brother has been dying for a taste of your sweet honey. Has anyone ever feasted on you, my lovely lady?" Daniel flicked her nipple with his tongue and drew another moan.

She shook her head no and Grant growled. "We have so much to teach and show you." He buried his

My Sugar Daddy

face into her pussy, eating it like a starving man. He smiled, hearing Laura plead for relief but not knowing what she was asking for.

"Come for my brother, sweet Laura. Let him feel you quiver around his tongue." Daniel spoke to her, the dirty talk increasing her arousal. She was on the verge, but not yet there. "Another finger, Grant. Put another finger in her ass."

Her tiny scream was eaten up by his kiss. Daniel lifted her head, kissing her but not giving her time to think. Her body shook as the orgasm rolled over her.

"Take her to the bed. She's ready for us." Grant stood and unfastened her feet as Daniel broke the kiss, undoing the wrap around her upper body.

Careful of her injury, Daniel scooped her up into his arms and moved to the bed which had been turned down and was ready for them. He placed her in the center of the bed, following her onto it, where he helped her sit on top of him. "Put me in you, Laura, but try not to pull your stitches."

Holding her hips, Daniel helped her lift up over his straining cock. He knew he would stretch her—he was above average in length and girth, which was one of the reasons Grant would take her ass first.

"God you're huge, nothing like…" She stopped and looked down at him. "Sorry. I didn't mean to compare."

Sitting up, she sank the rest of the way onto him and moaned as he wrapped his arms around her. "I understand he was your first and we'll be your last. It's normal, but from now on try to leave the little weasel out of it." He nipped her lip before lowering back down on the bed, bringing her down with him.

Behind them, Grant moved in, his cock covered and lubed.

"Stop! I need a condom." Daniel had totally forgotten. And now was not the time to get her pregnant.

"Daniel, I swear…" Grant snarled as Daniel reached over to the nightstand and ripped the package open.

"Sit up baby, for one minute, and let me put this on." She smiled and took the condom from Daniel's hands, lifting her body.

"Let me do this," she whispered and leaned down kissing his engorged dick before gently rolling the condom on it. "Thank you, Daniel," she said and covered him once more. This time she leaned down, placing her hands on both sides of Daniel's face as she stared into his eyes. "Someday we'll have enough little ones running around, but until we're settled we should wait."

It was the first time either of them had heard her talk about a future with them and it shocked both of them.

"You accept us?" Grant whispered behind her as he worked his cock into her ass. Her nails dug into Daniel's shoulders and he welcomed her marks of love.

"I am yours," she panted and reached behind her to circle Grant's neck, bringing him down for a quick kiss. "I too watched you tonight, and from what I witnessed, I knew I belonged here."

That was all it took. Both men moved inside her. One would pull out while the other pushed in. Daniel captured her mouth with his and their tongues dueled as the shyness evaporated from her. It was as if a light exploded for all of them.

He moaned and broke the kiss. "What—" was all he got out before a little flicker of lights surrounded them.

Surging into her, his seed erupted. Never had his control been totally obliterated, but he wasn't the only one. Grant snarled and stiffened above them and his gaze met Daniel's.

"Magic!" the brothers said at the same time and fell back onto the bed sideways, careful of the precious bundle between them.

Daniel knew this was only the beginning of their journey. Laura had many surprises in store for them, and he for one couldn't wait to unwrap each and every one.

Chapter Ten

Max's whimpers woke Laura. At first, she was disoriented and couldn't remember where she was until Grant leaned over and kissed her nose. "I'll get the bottle. You can change him." Grant rose from the bed.

Even in the dark, Laura had excellent vision, and the sight of his ass was enough to drool over. "Damn, you have a fine ass," she said, stretching and forgetting about the stitches. She sucked in her breath "God, I hate this."

"Well if you weren't staring at my brother's ass, you'd have been more careful," Daniel said behind her.

"Oh, shut up," Laura grumbled and made her way into the baby's room. She smiled down at her little man. "How's Mommy's little bundle? You're up early." Laura looked up to see the sun rising over the mountain.

"Well crap, it looks as if you slept the whole night." She unsnapped his sleeper and threw it over the side of the crib. "Might as well get you dressed. You're going to be up for a few hours now."

By the time Grant came into the nursery holding

My Sugar Daddy

the bottle, Laura had Max changed and dressed. "Good, you can feed him while I get dressed." She placed the squirming child into Grant's arms.

"What? It's too early. No one is up this early," Grant grumbled and sat in the rocker. He jumped back up, glaring at her. "We're getting a cushion for that seat." He grabbed one of the baby blankets and threw it over the wooden chair.

She laughed so hard her sides hurt. "What's wrong? Your cute ass get a cold shock?" she teased and moved into the bedroom where Daniel watched from the bed.

"You know he's going to get even with you. Why are you getting dressed? It's only seven." Daniel sat up and watched her step into the closet.

"I usually get up early. Plus, Max won't go back to sleep now—he slept through the night." She reached for the dark-blue dress and slipped it over her head. Laura would be glad when they could remove the stitches. Some days she just wanted a pair of jeans and a nice big sweater—her comfort clothes.

"You're a morning person, aren't you?" Daniel groused, coming up behind her and spooking her.

"Don't do that. You scared the crap out of me." Laura smacked his chest and took a deep breath. "You'd think with you guys in the service, you'd sleep in." Laura placed a kiss on his chest.

"Have you ever heard of morning woodies?" Daniel rubbed his cock against her and she laughed.

"Down boy. We don't have time." Laura escaped his grasp. "Go back to bed. You guys are going to be busy later on and need your rest."

She stepped into the nursery to find Grant talking

to Max while he fed him. "Your mommy is safe now, little guy. I promise no one will hurt her while we're around." Grant kissed the top of Max's head before turning to grin at her.

"You can't promise that, Grant. All you can do is try to. I'm happy with that. Give me the little guy and you go back to bed." Laura reached to take Max.

"I'm staying up. I need to make some calls before everyone gets moving around here." He stood and swatted her butt. "And for your information, I'll keep that promise. I'll meet you downstairs in a minute." Grant slipped into their bedroom and said something to Daniel, but Laura couldn't make it out.

"Let's go find some coffee." She placed a blanket over her shoulder and started to burp Max on the way down the stairs.

Coming off the stairs, Laura turned the corner and ran smack into a hard chest and screamed.

Someone reached for her, but Laura was turning already, trying to protect Max as she landed on the hardwood floor on her shoulder. "Son of a bitch!" Max was crying and Laura was pretty sure she'd just ripped opened the stitches on her side.

"Are you okay? I'm so sorry! I didn't think you guys would even be up," Rafe was there by her side as Grant and Daniel came running down the stairs half dressed.

"She ran smack into me. I tried to grab onto her, but she pulled away and I couldn't catch her," Rafe was explaining as Alex came running into the room in a T-shirt.

"Take Max, Alex." Laura released Max into Alex's arms and turned over to see a quarter-sized spot of blood on her dress. "Shit."

My Sugar Daddy

"Move your hand, Laura, and let me see what you've done. Rafe, get Seth in here with his bag." Grant tried to lift her dress and she glared at him. "Daniel, hand me that blanket over there."

"What were you told about this before?" Grant snapped before he placed the blanket over her legs and inched it up as he lifted her dress.

"Shut up already and help me up. I'm fine. It just hurts a little." Laura tried to move but flinched.

"What happened?" Seth said, coming into the room and moving to Laura's side.

"She fell and pulled the stitches open," Daniel grumbled behind her.

"Daniel, will you go and make some coffee for me? Because when I get up I'm going to need it." She again tried to sit up.

"Don't move." Seth pulled open his bag and pulled out what looked like a stapler.

"What are you doing with that?" Laura asked, trying to scoot away from him and that weird-looking thing.

"I'm putting staples in your side, since it's obvious the butterflies are not working. These won't pull apart as quickly. Grant, get on the other side and hold her still," Seth said.

She shook her head and pushed herself away from them both. "I don't think so." Laura kicked at Grant's hand when he wrapped his hand around her ankle.

"Hold still, you big baby." Grant placed his leg over hers and lay down next to her, holding her still.

His gaze held hers. "I'm right here and everything will be all right." Grant distracted her enough for Seth to get one staple in, and she could have sworn her side was on fire.

"Stop! That hurts!" Laura screamed and tried to get away, but they held her still as three more were put in place. Tears slid down her face and her nails were buried in Grant's arms as Seth placed a bandage over her wound.

"You're done, but I want you to take it easy today. Do not lift anything heavy." He looked at her son.

"Don't even say it," she snarled and slapped at Grant's hands, trying to get up. "Let go now, Grant."

Getting up, Grant reached down and lifted her, setting her on her feet. "I'll bring the stroller in the house," Grant started to say, but she wasn't hearing it.

"Come on, Alex, let's see if Daniel has the coffee going. Then, I'm going to finish feeding my son. The rest of you get lost, and Seth…" She turned to look at him. "You ever bring that wicked thing near me again, and I'll take a knife to your balls."

Their woman might act fierce, but Daniel could see she was in pain and favoring her side. He pulled out one of the kitchen chairs. "Sit. I'll get your coffee while you feed Max."

Laura nodded and sat slowly. She let the breath she was holding escape. "I don't know why I freaked out like I did. I knew there were others in the house. Sometimes I think my brain goes on vacation."

Alex leaned over and put a whimpering Max into his mother's arms. "It's okay, little guy. Mommy has you." Laura cooed to her son, rocking him gently and feeding him his bottle.

"Here's your coffee, baby, and don't worry. We

My Sugar Daddy

all have days when our brain leaves the station house." Daniel leaned down, kissing the top of Max's head. "I'm going to finish getting dressed. Please let Grant bring in the stroller, at least for today. If you want to hold him, we can put him in your arms. It's just the reaching that could pull at your injuries." He placed his hand on the back of her neck and squeezed gently. "By tomorrow you shouldn't be hurting as much, and I'm sure you'll be able to carry Max then."

"I hate this, but okay, tell the lug to get the stroller." She propped up the bottle and took a sip of her coffee and moaned. "I so needed that."

"Little moans like that should be declared illegal," Daniel grumbled, kissing her head.

The door flew open and would have hit the wall, but Daniel caught it first. "Mom, what are you doing up?" He frowned when he noticed her worried look.

"We need everyone up. If you're going into town, it needs to be now. One of those freak storms is brewing over the mountains. Your brother Roman said it's going to be bad."

"Shit! I keep forgetting about the weather here. Did you tell Grant?"

"Yes. Here is the stroller and I'm on my way to finish getting dressed. I suggest you do the same. I already have Rafe and Seth waking up the men. Seth is calling in extra medical supplies too, in case we need them. We'll all meet in the basement of the main house. It's big enough to hold us so we can plan from there." Grant leaned down and kissed his mom's cheek.

"Mom, I don't want Laura lifting anything today. She fell and Seth had to put staples in her side." As

Grant was explaining things to his mother, he moved to Laura's side and kneeled.

"Please, if you need something, ask us or someone who is around. We're going to be..."

She placed her finger on his lips and smiled.

"I promise to take care of myself because I know it will only worry you more, and right now we need you keeping everyone safe. Go. Eat something before you start your day."

"I'll check in later with you. Did you make a list for you and Max?" Grant placed a kiss on her head before standing.

"Yes, it's on the dresser upstairs. We'll be over in a few, as soon as Alex gets dressed and I find some boots." She frowned and lifted her bare feet.

"Hold it right there," Daniel said, and ran upstairs to grab the boots he had seen in the closet. His brother Roman had thought of everything, but it was strange he hadn't introduced himself to Laura.

Daniel grabbed the fur-lined boots, a pair of thick socks and was on his way out when he stopped in front of the nursery door. "Crap!" They needed winter gear for the baby.

"Okay, Roman, let's see if you thought of that too." Daniel mumbled as he stepped into the room and started to look around. Sure enough, a baby's winter snowsuit was hanging up behind the other door. "Amazing." He snatched the snowsuit and made his way down the stairs. Grant stood at the bottom of the stairs, talking to Seth.

Grant turned and noticed the items in Daniel's hand. "Why hasn't Roman come over?" Grant frowned and Daniel could have sworn he could see

Grant's brain working overtime. "Do you think?" Grant looked at him and Daniel knew what his brother was thinking.

"He always did talk about the triad. Was he preparing us?" Grant asked him.

Yes, they were different, and they still hadn't informed their woman. Daniel shrugged. "Could be. I'm sure we'll find out soon enough."

Daniel nodded as the man in question stepped into the house behind Grant. "It's about time. Is it true?" Daniel asked Roman, knowing he had heard what he said to Grant. Roman stood at seven two. Taller than everyone in their family and built like a runner, he was an albino which had always made him cautious around others.

"Hey Grant, we're going to need some winter stuff for Max," Laura said, coming out of the kitchen and moving to Grant's side.

"Our brother already thought of that." Daniel held up the small snowsuit and Laura took it out of his hand.

"Okay, who is this mystery man and how does he know my taste so well?" Laura held up the suit, but slowly put it down at her side as she noticed Roman for the first time.

"Oh my," Laura said, cocking her head to the side.

"Laura, this is our brother, Roman. He's the middle child and a pain in the ass," Grant said.

Nadine came into the room holding Max and watched as Roman stepped forward. Roman reached over and ran his finger down Laura's cheek. "Beautiful."

Trinity Blacio

Daniel could have sworn sparks flew just watching Roman touch Laura. "Well, that's settled. Roman, I suggest you move your belongings in here later today, but for now we need to hustle if we're going to get everything done before this storm hits".

He hated to break the sexual tension going on, but someone had to think straight.

And it was obvious both Grant and Roman were in a daze.

Chapter Eleven

The cooing sounds her son made had Laura smiling as she changed his diaper. The snowsuit was tucked into the stroller; she and Alex would be spending the day with Nadine.

"He's such a handsome little guy, and always smiling." Tracy leaned over the couch and tickled Max's belly.

"So, tell me, what do you think about all this Triad stuff? How's the rest of your family going to deal with it?" Laura asked Tracy.

Tracy snorted. "Honey, you have nothing to worry about. I think Roman has been preparing our folks for a while, but you're not the only woman in our family with three men. There is our Aunt Julie on my dad's side and then there is my sister Sandra, who'll be here later on. She's got two men, but…" Tracy leaned over and whispered in her ear. "Her men claim to be Skinwalkers."

Laura froze. Her mother had introduced her to a family of them when she was six. "Really? I met a few of them when I was small, but don't remember much."

Tracy's gaze was serious. "You should have seen my father when he found out. Do you believe in beings from other worlds?" Tracy handed Laura Max's shoes.

"Yes, there is no doubt about it. My mother and I used to talk about it." Laura smiled and leaned back. "We'd sit out under the stars at night and just talk. We both agreed, you'd have to be stupid not to. I mean to think we're the only intelligent beings among millions and millions of plants out there just sounds stupid, you know?"

"We are going to get along great, and you're right." Tracy handed her the other shoe. "I'll let you in on a little secret. I have this strange sense that the man I'm supposed to be with is out there." She pointed up. "And not here on this earth."

Before Laura could pick Max up, Tracy reached over and lifted him. "I've got him. You get your socks and boots on while I wrap him up in his blankets, then we'll head next door."

By the time Laura got herself and Max ready, the temperatures were already dropping. Alex opened the door and the cool air hit Laura. "Damn," she mumbled and drew the sweater around her tighter. "They'd better get me a coat, and soon."

The screech of an eagle had her looking up and waiting. Was it her mother? Laura stepped farther onto the sidewalk and watched as the great bird took a dive down toward her.

"Laura, watch out!" Tracy shouted, but Alex held her back.

"No, watch," she heard Alex whisper as the great bird landed on the fence post close to her.

"You knew about the Triad, the three brothers, didn't you?" Laura asked, stepping closer. She heard footsteps and knew the three men in question were behind her.

My Sugar Daddy

"Laura, step back slowly," Grant ordered, but she just waved her hand at him.

"It's fine, Grant. Mom's come to talk again, haven't you?"

The animal stared at her for a minute, before she heard her. "It's time for me to move on, my little girl. You are in good hands now. The three men behind you will take great care of you and Max. I love you, my little angel." With that, the bird lifted up and flew overhead.

"Momma, I love you." Tears rolled down Laura's cheeks as she watched the bird 'til she could see it no more. Strong arms wrapped around her from behind.

"You'll see her again. Your mother is a strong spirit and even the next world won't keep her from checking on you from time to time," Roman said, just holding her.

"For so long, it was just the two of us. It's as if a part of me is gone, but I'll be okay I have Max and now all of you." She turned and looked at Roman.

With all three men they were tall, but Roman was beyond tall. She felt like a child next to him, but his eyes were so expressive showed every emotion and way he stared at her made her feel so special.

"You are special to all of us. We might have just met, but our souls have known each other for a lifetime." Roman stepped back and held out his hand. "My lady."

Behind him, Grant and Daniel groaned. "He just has to pull that old-world crap," Grant grumbled and turned, moving back toward the main house. He stopped and looked at her over his shoulder. "Don't do that again, please. Those birds are known to attack."

"They won't attack her." Roman grasped her hand and followed Grant and Daniel. Tracy and Alex walked behind them, pushing the stroller. "Animals speak to her." Roman looked down at her. "You talk to the ground too, don't you?"

Laura shrugged. "I don't know if you would call it talking to the Earth. I know where to plant things and sometimes I can sense what the soil needs, but that's about all."

They stepped into the house, where Nadine and Richard were talking with two other men and a woman. "My sister," Tracy said from behind Laura.

"Hey squirt, when did you and the wolf boys get in?" Grant said hugging his sister and nodded to her men.

"We just got in, and from the looks of things, I'm glad I did. So that's her." The woman's gaze met Laura's, and at once Laura knew this sister did not like her.

Not one to hide, Laura stepped forward and held out her hand. "Hi, I'm Laura McGill."

"I know who you are," she snapped.

"Sandra, don't even start," Tracy stepped up next to Laura.

"Start what? Boy, does this bitch have you all fooled. Belinda told me all about her and how she seduced poor Warren. I hope you don't think my brothers are going to support your bastard son," Sandra yelled. She was so furious, spit flew everywhere as her men each grabbed an arm.

No one said anything for a minute as Sandra kept yelling. For the first time since coming there, Laura actually felt unwelcome. She heard Max's whimpers and turned.

"If you'll excuse me, I'll take Max back to the house," Laura said, and turned to see Alex ready to go off on the Sandra.

My Sugar Daddy

Walking toward Alex, Laura shook her head. "Come, we can work from the house next door. Plus, I was going to start the chili for tonight's supper. It will be easy for the men to dish out when they are ready to eat." She turned the stroller around and was ready to walk out, but Roman placed his hand on her arm.

"Please don't go," he said. "My sister doesn't have all the facts, or she wouldn't be saying these things. Plus, Mom has all the big pots here."

Laura looked over her shoulder to see Grant and Daniel following Sandra and her men out of the room.

"Laura's not going anywhere," Nadine announced and came over, hugging Laura tight. "I'm sorry about my Sandra. Please give Grant and Daniel time to talk to her. You'll see, she'll come around as soon as she knows the truth." Nadine frowned. "But you're right, chili would be great for tonight. We could make sheets of cornbread to go with it. Let me go check and see if we might need something from town. Alex, why don't you bring Max into the kitchen so we can put him in the playpen I've set up?" Nadine took Alex's arm, leaving Laura and Roman alone in the living room.

"Do you really believe she'll accept me?" Laura turned and looked up at Roman.

"My sister is like you. She trusts everyone and I'm afraid she's fallen for the bitch's lies, but once Sandra knows the truth she'll come around." His hands slid down to her ass and he squeezed her butt. "I can't wait to spend some alone time with you."

Roman lifted her to meet his gaze. "Give me a kiss, baby," he whispered before covering her mouth with his.

Electricity shot through her, or at least Laura

could have sworn that's what it was. She slid her arms around his neck, holding on as his kiss deepened.

He tasted of mint and coffee. Laura couldn't think as her back met the wall. This man knew how to kiss—she'd move one way and he'd counter it, keeping her right where he wanted her. Breaking the kiss, Roman placed his forehead against hers. "You are a hot little thing."

Lowering Laura so her feet touched the ground, Roman stepped back. Grant and Daniel were behind him. Both were smiling and shaking their heads. "Come on, lover boy, we have a room full of men we need to organize. Laura, Sandra has been given the facts and her husbands are staying with her 'til she calms down. I'm sorry about what happened," Grant came to her side and cupped her cheek.

"If I'd known she'd behave like this…" He looked down the hallway where they had taken her.

"It's not your fault, Grant. I just hope someday we can get along. It's going to be hard to be cooped up here with her if she hates me so much, but I'll try to stay out of her hair as much as possible."

"No. I've already told Sandra if she can't accept the truth, she will stay in her room. I will not have you stuck somewhere because she can't handle the truth." Grant kissed the top of her head.

"Roman, while we're in town this afternoon, maybe you and Laura can have lunch together and get to know each other better while Max takes a nap. You can set up the web cameras and such in the basement of our house, since we'll be using this one as a place we store some of our supplies. We need to get moving on the construction of another building and finish the plans for the new barn. Mom was right about it being a

My Sugar Daddy

perfect mess hall and a place for the men to bunk down in when we need them close."

Daniel watched Laura move into the kitchen after each of them had given her a kiss. For the next few hours, they would be buried in wires and meetings before heading into town.

Following his brothers toward the basement, Roman stopped and glanced over his shoulder. "Something isn't right."

A shiver went up his spine as Roman did an about face and started to move toward the kitchen. He looked at Grant and his brother shrugged, turning to follow him into the kitchen.

Once there, Daniel noticed Laura standing outside, her arms wrapped around herself, looking up at the mountains to the left. Roman moved to her side, engulfing her in his embrace. Daniel and Grant approached. "It's not a winter storm coming." She looked up at Daniel with tears rolling down her face.

"What do you mean it's not a winter storm?" Daniel asked as he brushed the tears from her cheek.

"She's partly right," said Roman. "There is a winter storm coming, but something man-made will be here first. We need to warn the townspeople now. Mom, are the propane tanks filled? Grant, we need to pull all the vehicles we have into the underground tunnels 'til this is over."

"EMP's," said Grant. Roman nodded. "I can't tell where they'll come from, but our enemy has already hit parts of the U.S. and Europe," Roman looked away for a minute.

"Maybe three hours," Laura said. "But are they nuclear?"

The sound of birds—lots of birds—drew their attention to the sky. Eagles, ducks, geese, all sorts of birds were coming in from the west. "No, not nuclear yet," Roman said. "There wouldn't be any animals coming from the west if it was."

All at once, they looked down at Laura. "Mom!" The three of them yelled. "I want you to take all the females down to the underground compound bringing whatever you can carry. I'll have a few men helping load up the supplies. Daniel, you stay with the women. Roman, I need you with me." Grant looked up to see Sandra in the door with her men behind her. "Don't start now," he snarled.

Sandra shook her head. "I can help. Please."

"It will be okay. You go do what you have to," Laura said, placing her hand on Grant's arm. "Just make sure you are back in time." Daniel turned and yanked her into his arms. Over her head, Grant looked at him. "Keep her safe. We'll be back in an hour. Looks as if Dad's crazy idea was a good one."

"I heard that!" his dad yelled and he smiled.

"Grant, get whatever medicine and canned things you can just in case we're underground for a while. You might want to get extra electrical parts to take down with us just in case things get burned up."

"We will. Now let's move," Grant yelled, running into the house and shouting orders as he went with Roman right behind him.

"Let's go, ladies. Laura, don't lift anything. I want you and Max in the bunker. You can help set things up as we bring them down," Daniel said.

"Alex, Alex, where are you, damn it?" Rafe and Justin yelled from inside the house. When they came outside and saw her, they relaxed.

My Sugar Daddy

Alex rolled her eyes and slapped at their hands. "Go do what you have to. I'll be fine," she snapped. As they tried to kiss her, she yanked herself out of their arms. "I told you there would be none of that."

Ushering Laura and Max toward the back of the house, Daniel heard Rafe snarl. "We'll finish this later."

"No, we won't," Alex yelled and came running up next to them. "Maybe I should leave." She sighed and followed Laura down into the tunnels.

Laura was already shaking her head. "Nope, you're staying, so get used to it. Plus, there is nothing left back at home. Your house is gone, as is mine. Now we can have the new start we wanted." Laura took her friend's hand. "We all have to learn to leave our baggage behind."

"You're one to talk. Have you told them?" Alex covered her mouth at the last minute, looking at him.

"Alex, if I didn't love you, I'd deck you right now," Laura said and looked over her shoulder at Daniel.

"We'll talk later," Daniel said, wondering what Laura hadn't told them.

"No time to worry about that now. Get them settled and start loading the bunker. I got a call from the general. New York, Texas, Cleveland and California have all been hit with EMP's. The same with Paris, London and Rome. Not only have these new associates of Hager's given him access to EMP's, they are more organized, and their numbers are bigger than anyone counted on."

Daniel pressed in the code and the wall opened up allowing them to enter. Both Laura and Alex gasped, looking around. "This side of the tunnels will hold more than 1000 men and women," he said. "There is another set of tunnels on the other side of the property. They will hold another 1000. My father and grandfather planned this and when Grant, Roman and I heard about them, we started adding things we knew we would need. Also, we started making it bigger. Eventually, we want to build an underground town down here. Come, I'll show you where the storage areas and our separate quarters are. Laura, I'll need you to point out to the men where everything should go and to keep track of what comes in. Alex, I need you to make sure Laura doesn't lift anything, and help her when she needs it. Mom will be coming down to open up the kitchen down here in a few. As soon as we get what we can down here for supplies, you two can help her there," Daniel said, showing them to first to their personal rooms, then to the storage areas.

"I'll get the heat moving in here too, but please stay safe." Daniel kissed the top of Laura's head before turning and heading for the control room.

Daniel ran the rest of the way through the tunnel to the control room. He punched in the passcode and flipped the lights on as soon as he entered. "Laura and Alex are both set," he barked into the phone. "Tell the men to start bringing in the supplies I'll have the doors open for the vehicles in a minute. I'm here activating the lifts now." Daniel opened the cargo bay doors to allow the cars, trucks and off-road machines to enter.

Daniel was glad he and his brothers had installed the new security cameras and alarms. Daniel turned on the cameras, making sure the one in the storage room was on so he could keep an eye on Laura.

Laura turned around in a circle. He could see a

grin on her face and Alex was laughing. Laura spun once more before turning to the camera and lifting her dress to show him her ass.

Daniel laughed so hard he swallowed the wrong way, almost choking.

Chapter Twelve

Flipping her dress down, Laura grinned as Alex wiped the tears from her eyes. "You are so bad," Alex said, leaning over and putting Max's pacifier back into his mouth.

"With everything going on around here, we need to laugh," Laura nodded to the camera. "They're putting their lives on line to protect us and everyone around us. So, tell me what's going on with you and those three hunks." Laura eyed Alex before pointing to the shelf as two men came in bringing supplies.

"Nothing. I told them to back off. I'm not sure I'm ready, Laura. Everyone I've loved has died—well, except for you, and I refuse to let go of you. So be warned, I will kick your ass if you get hurt." Alex looked around and waited 'til the men left for more supplies. "They have a right to know. When are you going to tell them?" Alex asked and patted the seat next to her. "Come rest for a few."

Laura sat down and propped her feet on the tires in front of them. "I had planned on telling them before our world went to hell. I didn't want to get serious with them until they knew." She looked down at her hands. "I might not tell them. I want children, so why even bring it up?"

My Sugar Daddy

"Because you have big babies and you have a hard time delivering them. Damn it, Laura, I almost lost you when you had Max. You can have C-sections—you'll just have to plan them." Alex nudged her with her shoulder. "Now tell me, how do you feel about having three men claiming you? Little weird, isn't it?"

She shook her head. "No, what's weird is having a man around at all. Going from doing everything myself and depending on no one, to having three of them suddenly wanting to do everything for me." Laura sighed. "I'm afraid to get used to it. Hell, I'm still having a hard time with losing my mom." She got up and nodded to the six men carrying in supplies.

Looking over each load, Laura was pointing to where things went when she noticed Sandra and her men coming into the storage area carrying supplies. At once, Alex was in front of her. "I'll handle this. Go sit down."

"I'll be fine, plus we're bound to run into each other anyways." Laura nodded to the sister at hand.

"Bodyguard?" Sandra asked, looking at Alex.

"No, just a true friend who would put her life before mine." Laura pointed to the shelf designated for the blankets. "You can put those over there."

"I know where they go, but thank you, and you don't have anything to worry about. I won't attack you. Just don't hurt my brothers."

Before Laura could stop her, Alex stepped into Sandra's path. "Let me tell you something about your bitch friend. Did you know she sent goons after Laura? That Laura was knocked out, had three broken ribs and almost lost the baby? Or the fact that her weasel of a husband was not only fucking Laura, but his secretary too?"

"Alex!" Laura yelled and slapped her hand over her friend's mouth. "She does not need to know all the gory details. Sorry." Laura shoved Alex back to the stroller and glared at her.

"What? She needed to know." Alex glared right back.

"Laura." Sandra was behind her.

She slowly turned around and stepped back. "Yes." That was when she noticed Daniel and Roman running into the room.

"I wanted to apologize for earlier. Daniel and Grant showed us the police reports and the hospital files. I should have known something wasn't right when Belinda showed up at my door last week. I hadn't seen her since school, but what she told me... Well, I was scared for my brothers."

"I don't like the fact Grant and Daniel showed you my file," Laura said. "It's my life we're talking about. It might not be pretty, but it's still all I have. You grew up with brothers and a sister. All I had was my mother until Warren came around. I couldn't believe a man like him would even want me. Believe me, Sandra, I had no idea about his wife." Laura glanced at Daniel and Roman.

Both men stood behind Sandra. "All I can promise you is that I'm trying to take it slow, but you know your brothers. It's like fighting bulls. Their way or no way."

Sandra snorted. "They're pigheaded, just like my dad, but again, I'm sorry. Maybe later we can talk." She looked at Alex. "All of us. I know it can be hard to adjust to more than one man. Maybe I can help?"

"That would be great for Laura, but I don't have

My Sugar Daddy

any men." Alex said and crossed her arms, glaring at Rafe, Bo and Justin as they carried in supplies.

Laura laughed. "If they're anything like Grant and Daniel, you're in trouble. I have no idea what Roman is like yet." Laura looked at Sandra, who was shaking her head, laughing.

"Sorry, Roman is worse than Grant." Sandra slapped Roman's hand when he tried to pull her hair. "What? I'm just stating a fact." Sandra laughed and ran into one of her men's arms. "Save me."

He laughed. "Not a chance. I'd be lucky if he didn't turn me into a toad or something. Come on, we have to get our things down here before they close off the compound."

"I heard you like others to watch?" Roman said, stepping up to Laura and sliding his hand into the top of her dress. He leaned forward and nipped her ear. "Many of the men love the two-way mirrors we put in the rooms, too."

"Roman, what are you doing?" Laura rubbed her legs together and tried to step back, but he wrapped one arm around her waist and held her still. "Lunchtime, little bug." He pinched her nipple and covered her mouth with his.

Roman was definitely just as domineering as his brothers, but there was also a slightly dangerous aura around him. Her body hummed as if charged when he touched her and by the time his kiss was over, Laura had to hold onto him 'til the room stopped spinning. "You are lethal." She fanned her face. "Can you really turn someone into a toad?"

He threw his head back and laughed. "That, my dear, will be answered another time. I have to go.

Grant is waiting for me. Be good." He slapped her ass and moved toward the door.

She glared at his back. "I swear that is the second time…" She stamped her foot and moved her gaze to Daniel. "What?"

He crossed his arms over his massive chest. "Getting a little snippy, aren't we?"

Counting to ten, Laura turned away from Daniel and focused on Alex. The three brothers hadn't seen her temper yet and now was not the time to display it. "Alex, will you watch things here? I'm going to go prepare Max's bottle."

Her friend, having the good sense not to argue, said, "If you bring it back here, I'll feed him for you."

"Thanks. I just need time to think." Laura pushed her hair out of her face before moving out of the storage room.

"Ignoring me isn't going to help," Daniel said behind her.

"I'm not ignoring you. I just need some time alone. You three come on like a sudden storm and leave me no room to think or to adjust." Laura stopped and glanced over her shoulder at him. "I know the three of you are used to getting what you want and you want to take care of us, but this was supposed to be about sex…not emotions."

Daniel wrapped his arms around her waist, careful of her staples as he held her against his body. His gaze captured and held hers. "You are like an owl, carefully considering each strike before actually moving in, but there is no need for that, Laura. That is what we have been trying to tell you." He placed a kiss on her forehead.

My Sugar Daddy

"I know it's asking a lot, going from doing everything yourself to allowing us to taking care of you, but we are very good at it," he said.

"How am I supposed to think when you three are always touching me and keeping me in a state of sexual frustration?" Laura rested her forehead on Daniel's chest and took a deep breath. She loved his scent. "How can this be right? Aren't you pissed off at having to share me? I'm just so confused."

The moment Laura stepped into his arms, Daniel knew she'd allow him to help her. He smiled and kissed the top of her head. She had a temper, but Laura kept a tight rein on it. Now was not the time to bring it out.

"No, Laura. Grant and I always knew we would share. Roman was the quiet one, but over the last year or two, Grant and I both knew our younger brother would be connected somehow. He kept calling us the Triad brothers—that we would need to be together for what was going to come." He stepped back and placed his hands on either side of her face.

"Did we know we would be sharing you? Yes. Are we upset? No. How could we be? He's another part of the whole. The four of us are one unit. We can't survive without each other. I see that now and so do my brothers. I know things are moving fast and we'll expect many things from you, Laura, but you were meant to be ours."

"I believe you, but did Roman have to leave me…well you know?" Her cheeks turned a little pink.

"Don't you think he was needy too? With everything going on, we have to put those feelings on hold until we're all safe. Tonight, we will take care of you, I promise. Now go get Max's bottle. Mom is in the kitchen and she has it ready for you. Alex will meet you there with Max. Sandra and her men are going to take Alex's spot since she can't cook worth a damn."

Laura laughed. "I'm sorry. I didn't mean to be such a pain. Go. I know you have work to do too."

"I do, but first let me help you," Daniel purred as he slid his arm around her back and held her still against the wall of the tunnel. "We can't have you suffering now, can we?"

With his other hand, Daniel slid it under her dress to her pussy. "Spread your legs for me, darling, and allow me to take the edge off." Before she could say anything, Daniel dropped his knees in front of her.

"I need an early treat." Daniel lifted her legs over his shoulders and licked from her ass to her pussy.

"What are you doing?" Laura grabbed onto his head and moaned the last word as he slid his tongue into her wet cunt. Daniel would never be able to get enough of her. His nose rubbed against her clit, driving her closer and closer, and when Daniel knew Laura was ready, he pulled her clit into his mouth and slid three of his fingers inside her.

"DANIEL!" Her legs shook on his shoulders. He kept pumping his fingers until another smaller orgasm settled over her.

Kissing her labia, he slowly lowered her legs to the ground, all the while holding her and making sure she wouldn't fall.

Her eyes slowly opened and then frantically looked around them.

"There is no one here. Can you stand?"

My Sugar Daddy

She nodded, still trying to get herself under control.

"I have to go now, sweet thing. You remember how to get to the kitchen?" he asked her, but Laura was still in a fog. "Never mind. Come on, I'll take you. I don't want you to get lost." With his cock hard and rubbing painfully against his pants, Daniel guided Laura down the tunnel with the stroller.

"Daniel?"

Her voice held a little uncertainty but she continued. "Thank you, but you were going to tell me something about your brother, weren't you?"

"Yes. As you know, Roman is an albino. That's why his skin and hair are the way they are. But there are also other things about my brother, things that make it necessary we always protected him best as we can." Daniel stopped before the kitchen doors and smiled down at her. "Let's just say my brother is rather large and it's going to be a little painful at first when you take him."

She frowned. "Large how? I mean, the both of you are not normal. At least I don't think so, but then again I've only been with the asshole." Laura cocked her head to the side and smiled.

He laughed and tapped her nose. "Don't say I didn't warn you. Now, I have to go. You be good and we'll see you at lunch." He planted a gentle kiss on her lips and turned to leave.

His cell phone rang as he did. "We're here in town," said Grant. "The general is here along with the rest of the teams. I've instructed them to drive right to the compound. It seems Grandfather wasn't the only one who was worried—beneath this town there are three different bunkers. The sheriff is sending out men now to bring in those who are farther out."

Daniel turned the corner to see his youngest brother coming toward him with his father. "We've moved all the meat and food supplies down below. The animals are being rounded up and taken to the concrete barn now," Haden announced joining him as they turned the corner to the control room.

"The TV is gone—just the emergency broadcast signal is on now and the same for the radio," his father said, pushing open the door to the control room. "But we do have this and I've placed antennas all throughout our property." He lifted a large tarp to show off his CB system.

"Thanks, Dad. We should make sure someone listens who can decipher what we might pick up." Daniel worked the buttons of the newer control panel. "See these?" He pointed to the 12 security monitors above them. "The one on the left top row is Times Square, the one in the top middle is Washington, D.C. Right one is our own town, followed by these three in the middle row. The bottom three are around the house and the grounds. Each camera is protected from EMP's, everything."

Grant's voice sounded in Daniel's ear. "Daniel, the general is going to be staying with us. He has the link to the president and our compound is now headquarters. We have the supplies and the rest of the men are now sealing off the town. They'll finish the barricades when the rest of the families arrive. I'm on my way back with the general. When the town is secure, the rest of our men will join us. I have 20 men who agreed to stay with the civilians." His brother

My Sugar Daddy

growled the last part. "Rafe, Justin and Bo are with them."

"What?" Daniel said out loud, furious they chose to stay and not protect Alex.

"I'll explain when I get there." Grant broke off their connection.

"What's wrong?" His father and brother quickly looked at him then back at the monitors. The one in Times Square was bad. Chaos wasn't even a good word for it. People lay dead in the street, buildings were burning and people were acting crazy.

"There will be nothing left. In a way, your woman has saved our family. Your mother would have been downtown working," his father said, staring at the screen.

"I take it this can be expected in the other cities?" Haden asked. He nodded.

"Martial law will be enacted now," Daniel said. "I'm sure every branch of the service has been called in. We'll learn more when Grant gets here. The general will be staying here." Daniel looked up at the monitor and realized his father was right. If he and Grant hadn't gone after Laura, they could have lost part of their family today.

"Did Granddad and Grandma make it here? What about Marc? Wasn't he in New Mexico?" Daniel asked his father and he nodded.

"My parents are here. Your brother was on his way here as of yesterday, but I haven't heard from him yet. Marc last checked in when he landed in Bangor two hours ago."

"He'll make it here. You know nothing can stop Marc when he sets his mind to something." Plus,

Daniel knew his SEAL training would help him if he ran into any trouble.

On the bottom monitor, Daniel noticed the ten, M931A2 DOOMSDAY 5 Ton MONSTER Military 6x6 Cargo Truck Tractor pulling into the compound garage, followed by six A2 Turbo Trucks loaded with men and supplies.

"Grant should be right behind these men. We'll be able to see where we stand now." Daniel stood and went over to the small fridge grabbing a bottle of water. By tonight, hopefully they would know what to expect.

Chapter Thirteen

Laura placed Max in the playpen Nadine had set up. For the next two hours they laughed and talked, all the while fixing mass amounts of food for the men who were coming in.

Tracy announced there were close to 1000 men split up between the two bunkers underground. Laura took a deep breath and scanned the restaurant-like kitchen. Everything was done in stainless steel. The fridges were so big two people could easily walk into them at the same time. Not to mention the freezers were as big as the room she was standing in.

Never had Laura seen so much food in one place—rows of all kinds of meats, frozen vegetables and meals already made. Nadine was a powerhouse and she had been ready for this day, which surprised Laura more.

Could Laura be like Nadine? Always ready to leave at the last minute in case something was to happen? She thought about it and nodded. Even though they had been busy and it had been crazy, Laura never felt more alive than here. In her little apartment, it had been a struggle to just get up and make it through the day, but so far Laura had never felt more at home since her mom was alive.

"Earth to Laura!" Alex waved her hand in her face and laughed when she jumped. "Where were you, or do I even want to know?" she teased.

She snorted and pushed Alex out of the way. "I was just thinking that if I was back in my apartment, I would be trying to figure out how to make ends meet. Just surviving." She opened the oven and took out the next two batches of cornbread and placed two more large pans inside the stove. "But here, it's as if I'm alive for the first time since Mom died. I have a purpose—not that Max isn't a purpose, but you know." She looked at her best friend and she nodded.

"Yeah, I was thinking the same thing. Look at her." Alex nodded to Daniel's mom. "How does that woman do it? I mean, she's amazing. Knows everyone's name, can remember recipes and knows where everything is in this huge kitchen. Plus, she's not freaking out that God knows what is going on out there, and keeping us from doing so."

Nadine turned and faced them both. "Believe me, it's not easy, and after 30 years of taking care of all these kids, a few more people is nothing. But I do have my days and when that happens, Richard is there." Nadine's face held a faraway look. "He knows when I just need to be held or to give me space. Not once do I have to worry about having enough shampoo or soap. The little things are taken care of so I can do what is more important—take care of my family."

Nadine grinned and turned her attention back on Laura. "My sons are just like their father. You won't have to ask for anything, because they'll know what you need. Don't get me wrong, I fight with Richard. Being possessive and having someone watch your

My Sugar Daddy

every move can be annoying. He's gotten better, but when you have men like him, alpha and dominating us, women must learn to cope if we want to stay in their lives. You'll never find better men."

A shadow fell, blocking the light before Laura felt the warm breath on her neck. "I don't know what smells better, this kitchen and the food or you," Grant mumbled around her neck. He placed tiny kisses on her skin as he pushed the sleeve of the dress aside.

She turned in his arms and looked up at his handsome face. "Is everyone back from town? What's going on? Do we really have to stay under here?"

He kissed her nose. "The general is here with us. We'll be talking with him over lunch. That's one of the reasons I'm here. Can you and Mom bring us some food in the control room? We'll eat through lunch. There will be ten of us total."

"Do you know where Rafe is? He was supposed to bring the rest of our things down and I haven't heard from him, Justin or Bo," Alex asked coming over to them.

His body stiffened in her arms and Laura knew it wasn't good news. "Your things are in the room right across from our room. Rafe, Justin and Bo have volunteered to stay in town to help with the townspeople. They'll be bunkering down with them in their underground safe rooms."

Laura turned to her friend who held up her hand. "Don't. I knew they weren't serious about me. Thank you for making sure my belongings were there and putting me next to Laura. Now, if you'll excuse me, I have to stir the chili pots."

As soon as Alex was away from her, Laura glared

up at Grant. "You two promised me they wouldn't hurt her!" Not giving him time to say a word, Laura followed Alex's footsteps and hugged her friend from behind.

"We'll be fine," she whispered and hoped what she said was true.

"Alex," Grant called to her friend from behind them. Laura and Alex turned to look at him.

"Rafe, Justin and Bo knew you would be safe here with us. It's the only reason they volunteered. You have to understand, there is an orphanage in the town." Grant ran his hand through his hair.

"I shouldn't be telling you this, but Rafe was raised in one and it wasn't good. When he noticed the home…well, he couldn't leave the children, and neither could the others who stayed."

"Thank you, Grant, that explains a lot to me." Alex patted his arm and smiled at her. "I'll be okay. At least there is a reason other than me. So, I can hope."

Before Alex could turn away, Grant handed her an envelope. "Rafe wrote this real quick for you."

"Go help Nadine. I'll be fine." Alex pushed Laura away before ripping open the letter.

"I'll see you at lunch?" Grant asked, drawing Laura's attention.

"I want to be there. I need to know what is going on." Laura pivoted to help Nadine, but once more Grant captured her around her waist.

"We'll watch out for her. They are committed to Alex—you'll see. If I have to, we'll bring the kids and them back here. I won't let you down," Grant promised before swatting her butt and leaving her there, stunned.

My Sugar Daddy

"You know it is something to think about, bringing those children here. I mean we are surrounded by men. What better place to protect them?" Nadine said as she pulled out a steel rolling cart.

The doors to the mess hall swung open and Tracy and Sandra came in with two other women. "We're set up," Tracy said, grabbing two of the racks of cornbread while Sandra and the women grabbed the bowls, chili and butter.

The drinks were already in the room. They had made pots and pots of coffee. Of course, Laura was now zinging along on a caffeine buzz.

Placing a bowl in front of her, Nadine pointed. "Sit. We'll eat here first. I'm sure they are setting up the tables in the control room and getting settled." Nadine grabbed herself a bowl and handed one to Alex as she stepped up.

"So, what did the letter say?" Laura asked, taking a bite of the chili and moaning.

"More or less what Grant had said, but I still think they're giving me the time I asked for, which is fine." Alex also moaned when she took a bit of her chili. "This is amazing."

"It is good. You were right, Laura, the turkey hamburger adds just the right touch. Plus, it will save on the hamburger. We'll have to have the men go hunting soon too. I want to add deer meat and some wild birds in the freezer."

Nadine tapped her fingers on the pad of paper she'd pulled out. "Can you think of anything else?" She looked at them both.

"Well, we used to have turtle soup. If you have lakes, there are bound to be snapping turtles," Alex added.

Trinity Blacio

"There are rabbits, but they don't give much meat," said Laura. "I think the best things would be the birds, deer, any wild hogs too. I just hate the thought of killing all those animals."

"Then let's pray this thing gets settled before anything else happens, but right now I think we better stick to raising our own cattle and such," said Nadine. "I'm also thinking we should board up our well supply, protect it. You never know if they will want to strike against our food supply."

"You need to have the men find some underground water supplies. How far is the town from here?" Laura asked, eating the last bite of her chili.

"If you're driving, about 20 minutes, but you can't go there now." Nadine eyed Laura and Laura laughed.

"No, I was just thinking it might not be a bad idea somehow if we can connect the town's bunkers to the tunnels you have," said Laura. "One, it would give another escape route if need be, and we could share our resources. The more people we have helping, the better we'll be."

"You're right," said Nadine. "We'll bring that up when we serve them lunch. Let's check and see how the chili is holding out in the mess, then we'll head to the control room." Nadine stood, taking her dish to the sink.

"You two go to the control room. I'll stay here and keep an eye on Max. He's sound asleep—there's no sense in waking him." Alex finished her lunch and reached for her coffee.

"Are you sure? You're going to get sick of watching him," Laura teased and Alex laughed.

My Sugar Daddy

"Never! Now let's get this cart loaded while Nadine loads the mess hall up." It took them 15 minutes to make sure everything was filled and ready to go. Nadine pushed the cart since Laura had no idea where they were going.

"Warning you right now—the general is a jackass, so be prepared. I've had the displeasure of meeting him a few times and I was not impressed."

"Great, just what we need around here," Laura mumbled and Nadine agreed. One thing was for sure—there were a lot more hot men in the complex.

"Well we aren't going to be without eye candy, are we?" Laura said, forgetting for a second who she was talking to as her gaze followed a few men walking by.

"Hell no, but don't let my sons catch you staring. If they're anything like their father, they'll be very jealous." Nadine laughed and even nudged her when two other soldiers walked by.

"What would you two be looking at?" They both jumped at the sound of Roman's voice. His mother laughed until she spotted her husband right behind Roman. "Well shit."

Daniel watched as his mother and Laura came into the control room with their lunch. Grant stood and pulled Laura into his arms. "You're not out of the woods yet, dear," Grant whispered in her ear before turning her to meet the general.

"General, this is our woman, Laura McGill. Laura, this is General Liam Teeter. He'll be staying here with us while we work at getting everything back to normal."

She held out her hand to Teeter, but the way he

Trinity Blacio

looked at Laura sent up warning signals. Daniel never did like the guy.

Teeter took her hand into his and kissed the top of it. Daniel was ready to punch the guy when he said. "You must be something to hold three men's interest, my dear." His gaze raked down her body as Laura snatched her hand back.

Grant kissed the side of her neck. "Why don't you help Mom while I have a word with the general?" He nudged Laura over where Nadine was speaking with his dad and brother Haden.

Standing, Daniel stepped behind his brother, knowing this was going to be interesting. "General, if you ever disrespect our woman again, you'll find your ass outside and fending for yourself." Grant leaned forward, his hands in fists at his sides. "I've already apprised the president of your attitude and the only reason you are here is because of your knowledge of this group who has joined Hager. So, I really suggest you watch yourself."

The small man leaned forward, almost in his brother's face. "You do know, I could have you court-martialed for talking to me like that."

"No, you can't, but I can." Grant opened a file on the table and shoved it toward the man. "I was going to hold off showing this to you, but now there seems to be no point in waiting."

Looking over his brother's shoulders, Daniel frowned. "What is it?"

"The president knew the general was unfit to serve. The only reason he's here is because it's his last chance and if he screws this up, he loses everything. Pension, all of it. One word from me or anyone, and

My Sugar Daddy

he'll be brought up on charges. The president has had too many complaints about him." Grant looked at Daniel, then at Roman.

"She is not to be left alone while he is here," Grant said. "I have men who will be watching his every move. Also, he is not to know passwords or have anything to do with security."

"I don't understand this. How could the president do this to me? I've served him for the past seven years," the man snapped and sat down.

Taking his seat across from the general, Daniel leaned back in his chair and smiled up at Laura as she placed a bowl of chili and cornbread in front of him.

"There's fresh coffee, milk and I think your mom brought some iced tea too," Laura said.

"The tea would be great," Daniel said, squeezing her leg. She nodded and looked up at Grant.

"I'll have coffee. It's going to be a long day." Grant cupped her cheek.

Daniel couldn't take it anymore—the general's nasty looks at Laura were too much. Daniel stood and his chair went flying back. "Laura, honey, why don't you and Mom leave the cart here and we'll serve ourselves? I'm sure after all that cooking you'd like an hour or so to just sit back and relax." Daniel took her hands, raising them to kiss each one. "Plus, I know standing on your feet like this has to be pulling on your side." He looked at his mom.

"We'll come and help cook tonight," Daniel said, but Nadine was already shaking her head.

"There is no need. We have hams in the oven cooking now. Come on, Laura, let's go. Oh, here is a list of things we were talking about. You might want to consider putting some men on it." Nadine handed Grant her list and grabbed Laura's hand. "Come on, we'll get Alex and I'll show you my private retreat down here." They were walking out the door when Grant looked to Roman.

"No, I'll go. I've eaten and your grandfather can fill me in tonight," his father said, glaring at Liam. "I for one can't stand being in the same room as that man."

"Dad," Grant warned, but his father was already out the door, following the ladies.

"Let's get this over with. We have too much to finish before nightfall to be sitting here." Grant pulled his chair out as Roman followed his father out the door. One of them would stay with Laura now, since the little weasel sitting across him had a reputation for attacking woman.

"Okay, General, what do you know about this new group who has joined with Hager and why would they join him?" At first the man said nothing, but ate his lunch and watched the monitor.

"At last count, Tallen's little army was well over 10,000 men. If Hager promised him these EMP's or any other weapon, Tallen wouldn't hesitate in helping him. Not only is this man crazy, he believes everybody owes him. If I were Hager, I'd be watching my back." Liam reached over and poured himself a cup of coffee.

"Look, I apologize. I have this stupid problem when women are around. I can't keep my mouth shut." The general sat back, sipping his coffee. "Anyway, when I was leaving Washington, the groups in California and Texas had been neutralized, but the other two groups hadn't been. They used drones and

My Sugar Daddy

we're still trying to figure out how they did it. We brought one with us. We figured your brother Hayden would like to take a glance at." He moved closer to the table and looked at Grant.

"From what intel was gathered, we believe the biggest group is moving this way. They don't know where you are, but Hager knows you're in one of the northern states. Ever since you wiped out half of his men, including his brother, he's lost it. Of the group still alive, half of them left Hager, claiming he was suicidal and crazy."

"How do you know this?" Daniel could always tell a lie and this man wasn't lying about this.

"He might not like me and I'm an ass, but I will never betray our country. Your teams are the best we have. One of the men who left Hager was captured. He's talking like a bird. He also warned us he won't stop 'til he finds you, but, I have to say, that is not what has the president worried." He reached down and dug through his brief case before pulling out a file about an inch thick.

"This is all we have." The general looked at his watch. "This time tomorrow we'll have one more truck filled with others who want to see this man just as dead as we do. Their information is in here, but it goes no further than us. You can read over this tonight and we can meet in the morning before they arrive." The general stood and looked from Daniel and then to Grant, ignoring the others in the room.

"Only a handful of people know about this and the president has ordered all files on this destroyed except for what we are transporting here. He's ordered the rest of the information to come to you when it's safe. This will now be the secured location for any other survivors we find until we know more. Thank your mother and your woman for the food. It was great. I'll go to my room for now."

Grant waved his hand and two members of their team stepped up. "Take the general to the sixth wing. His room is B9. Make sure his fridge is filled with water." Both men nodded. Each had known ahead of time they were not to leave this man alone. Others would relieve them when the time was right, but the general was under 24-hour watch.

Every muscle in Daniel's body was tense. "Were there others? Did we forget someone?"

His brother shook his head.

"No, we went through that compound three times before we blew it," his grandfather said, squeezing Daniel's shoulder. "You won't know 'til you open the file."

With shaking hands, Grant opened the file. Grant's face had to be as white as his. There on the first page was written Genetic Code on Humans.

"Son of a bitch! I'll kill every last one of them!" his grandfather yelled, jumping up and throwing his cup of coffee at the wall, smashing it into pieces. "Haven't you boys been through enough?"

Chapter Fourteen

As soon as Laura stepped into the kitchen, she knew something was wrong. The tension in the air had shifted. Growls could be heard in the mess hall. Next to her, Nadine stiffened.

Nadine spun around and stared up at her husband. "What's happened?"

Before Richard could say anything, Roman answered for him as he surrounded Laura with his strong arms. "It seems we were not the only ones to have been experimented on. Another group of men are on their way here." Roman turned her around to face him.

"Grant and Daniel will meet us in our room. Grab Max." He looked up and over at Alex as he nodded. "Alex, you come too. You have the right to know. Mom, the general is being watched so you and the other women don't have to worry. We'll meet you back here in an hour or so."

Kissing the top of her head, Roman released Laura as she went to gather Max, but Alex was already there, picking him up. "You forgot again, didn't you?" She pointed her finger at Laura and Laura nodded.

"Yes, with everything going on my brain, and my

hormones are all over the place," Laura mumbled gathering up Max's binky blanket and a few of his toys. "Nadine, I'll just leave the playpen up, since we'll be back later." She turned to see Nadine gone and Roman there waiting.

"Dad took Mom to their room. She needs some time alone with him. I'm sure the playpen will be fine. All ready?" He looked at them both as she and Alex tucked Max into the stroller.

Alex pushed the stroller ahead of them as they walked through the tunnels. "This section is new, isn't it?" Laura asked, running her hand over the steel walls.

"Yes, all our personal quarters are in the newer section. We added more security, exit doors and other things the both of you will learn of eventually," Roman sighed. "There are things you'll see that you won't understand or might scare you. Just keep an open mind is all we ask."

She held out her hand and he took it. "We'll be fine. Alex and I know how to survive. We've done it enough."

In front of her, Alex snorted. "That's an understatement." She looked over her shoulder and winked. "But then again, we can get through anything as long as we have each other."

"That we can, my friend, that we can," Laura said as Roman reached around Alex and opened the door to their private quarters. Inside they had a sitting room with a fake fireplace, three bedrooms and a kitchen with a small fridge, warming plate, microwave and toaster. The only thing they were missing was a coffeepot and Laura was going to insist on that.

But all thoughts of the coffeepot vanished when

My Sugar Daddy

she stepped into the room and noticed Grant, Daniel, his grandfather, brothers and two of his team going through papers. Noticing them, they all stood up.

"We'll give you time and come back in say an hour?" Their grandfather asked. Grant nodded.

"Thanks, Granddad." Grant came over and scooped Max up into his arms. "How are you doing, little guy?" He held the baby up in the air and before Laura could warn him Max had just eaten, the baby upchucked.

The small stream of vomit landed square on his face. Grant held out the baby to Daniel as he used his shirt to clean himself off. Laura tried to hold her giggle back, but she couldn't, and burst out laughing. "I was going to warn you he'd just eaten, but you were too quick."

She was not the only one who was amused. Alex took Max and cleaned him up while Daniel and Roman struggled to stop laughing.

"Thank you, baby, we need that laugh," Daniel kissed her cheek and hugged her tight. "Please sit Alex. What we're about to explain to you is going to be hard to take."

After going into the bathroom, Grant came out with his hair wet and wearing only jeans a few minutes later. "Well, I'll never do that again." He winked at Laura before turning serious and sitting down across from her and Alex.

"About 20 years ago, my mom took Roman, Daniel and myself to New York. We were making a day of it and we'd just sat down in Central Park when all hell broke loose. Mom didn't know what to do. About 30 masked armed men came into Central Park and started grabbing people. Come to find out later they only took the children, including us."

She gripped Alex's hand and waited. They didn't have to wait long.

"It was a program called Genetic Codon Humans. The compound where they kept the three of us had over 60 children. These extreme scientists, as we called them, had captured a few other world species a few years before. Not only did they decide to kill and dissect the poor things, they took it a step further. They wanted to see what would happen if they spliced their DNA with human DNA. What better way to use children?"

"How long were you there? What happened?" Alex asked, the questions running through her mind, almost snarling.

"It took our father and grandfather six years to put together a team without the help of the government." Daniel looked at her. "Certain members of the government knew about it. When we were rescued, every member there was killed for what they had participated in."

Roman walked behind the couch and stood behind his brothers. "I wasn't always like this." He held out his arms. "Like Grant and Daniel, we have certain abilities." "What happened to the other children?" Laura asked.

"Our teams are made up of the children who were in that compound. Each one sought us out and has joined us. Over 65 men and women, each with different abilities—but all of us are connected now." Grant looked down at his hands.

At first, Laura thought Grant was just lost in

My Sugar Daddy

thought as he stared down at his hands. But when his skin started to turn a bluish-green color and a red diamond-type mark appeared on his hand, Laura looked up to see Grant's green eyes on her. "We'll keep you safe and you won't have to worry about anything if you don't want us now."

She looked to see Daniel was a darker-green color, but had no marking on his hand. "Why are you telling us this now? What's happened?"

Sliding a folder over, Grant opened it and the words in bold sent a chill down her spine. "There was another compound and there might be more. A truck will be here tomorrow with the survivors. Things are going to be crazy around here getting them settled. You need to be prepared for what's going to happen."

The questions were flying in her head, but Laura knew the three men who had claimed her were waiting. "One question. Do you think it is because of what happened to you that you are attracted to me? Because let's face, it I'm not your—" Laura didn't get a word out as all three men snarled and jumped up.

"Don't even finish that sentence. If you didn't have staples in your side you'd be over my knee right now," Grant snapped and glared at her.

"Then you should have known better to ask me the same thing, shouldn't you?" Laura stood and moved in front of Grant. She took the hand that held the diamond and kissed the center of it. All three men moaned.

"I am not superficial, Grant. So far, you have treated Alex and me with respect. You have protected us and you even care for my son. There is no other place I would want to be right now but with you, all of you."

"Okay. Like wow, it's getting warm in here," Alex said behind her, breaking the sexual tension. "I have a question. Have you or any of your team actually seen any of these aliens? Were they alive when you were there?"

"No, at least there was none alive in our prison facility." Daniel sat down and tugged Laura out of Grant's grasp, placing her on his lap.

"What's the diamond for?" Laura asked Grant as he sat next to them pulling her feet into his lap.

"Roman believes it's a sign of a leader among the others. We call the people others—it seemed better than alien or species." Grant looked toward the door just before someone knocked on it.

Grant's color returned to ivory, as did Daniel's, right before Roman answered the door. Two members of Grant's team came into the room. "Sir, we have a few visitors above," one man said before turning his gaze on her for second. "May we, sir?"

Daniel's body stiffened as he placed Laura on her feet and stepped in front of her in a protective manner. "Explain." Daniel snapped.

"Something happened. We were in the mess hall…" He ran his hand over his bald head. "It felt as if we're unified somehow. I wasn't sure until I saw her in your arms. She's sealed all of our bonds or something." The man looked at the other man and he nodded.

"We'll figure that out later. Right now, I want to know who these men are. Roman, do you sense anything?" Grant asked as he looked over his shoulder at his brother.

"No, let's go to the control room. We can spot them there." Roman was already headed there.

My Sugar Daddy

"Stay here. We'll be back." Daniel kissed her lips softly and followed Roman out the door.

Laura looked up at Grant in front of her. "You won't regret your decision. My men were right though—we are connected now, and I won't let you go, Laura." He traced his finger down the side of her cheek before he turned and left.

"Damn, woman, you four can sure heat up a room," Alex teased, placing Max in the stroller.

"It's not me, it's them," Laura sighed and plopped down next to Alex. "So much for taking things slow."

Laura stared down at the sleeping baby. It was still hard to believe Max was four months old. He had gotten so big in such a short time.

"I'd love to take a walk around the property up there. We never did get to see it," Laura said.

"You know that's not going to happen unless something changes. So, do we sit here and wait for them to come back?" Alex asked, getting up.

"Why don't we go exploring the tunnels? We've only been through a few anyway." Laura stood, frowning. "I'm going to change. Those hallways are drafty. I'll just throw on some sweats."

"Sounds like a good idea. I'll run next door and meet you back here," Alex said going to door.

Laura turned to say something, but stopped staring at the two strange beings in her doorway. Alex screeched and ran to her side. "Am I seeing things?"

The bluish-green men stepped into the room, staring at them. "Can I help you with something?" Laura had the feeling these were the two men who had been above.

"I am called Gresan and my partner is Evav. We're looking for the ones you have claimed," the taller one said in perfect English.

He was as tall as Roman, but lanky. Gresan spoke but he never moved his mouth. Both had black eyes and were bald.

"Don't anger them. We're on our way." Grant's voice echoed in her head, shocking her for a minute.

"Gentlemen, you might want to move away from the door," Laura said, and pointed to the chairs.

Evav nodded. Laura could have sworn there was laughter in his eyes. "Your men are very protective of you, but that's to be expected now that you are entwined." Evav frowned as he studied Laura. "They haven't finished yet."

Laura jumped and grabbed Alex when Grant came storming into the room snarling. Daniel and Roman were right behind him, followed by their family and men.

With all the commotion, Laura heard Max whimper and she glared at Grant. "Great, just freaking great, now he'll be cranky all freaking day. Thank you very much."

Daniel couldn't believe it. Laura was actually upset with him. All while two alien men were standing in their quarters. He stepped up behind her, placing his body between the men and her. "You're mad because we woke up Max?" he hissed in her ear as she placed Max's binky back into his mouth. "There are strange men in our room!"

Laura put her hands on his chest and tried to push him back. "You big oaf! If they wanted Alex or me, we would have been gone before you even got here. If they

My Sugar Daddy

could get inside here, they can go anywhere. They knocked on the damn door and didn't come in 'til I told them to move or get plowed over by all of you. So stop all the huffing and puffing. Find out why they are here." She frowned and glanced past him. "I think somehow they carry the same blood or something." Laura looked up at him. "Can't you feel it? There's like a hum, electricity or something. Something I've never dealt with."

Daniel covered her hands with his. "Right now, all I hear is my own heart beating fast and hard. That happened when we found out they were here." Daniel carefully picked her up and sat on the couch with her in his lap. "Come sit, Alex." Daniel patted the couch next to him.

Grant turned and looked at Laura. "She's fine, Grant," Daniel reassured his brother.

All eyes turned once more on the others standing in their room.

"Why are you here?" Grant wasted no time questioning them.

"We came searching for our brothers, but found them gone, and yet they are not." Gresan seemed to slide forward without even touching the floor. He was inches from Grant. Around them, their men moved in slowly, but Grant waved them back.

"You and each person who was altered carry part of our missing brothers. What happened?" There was a little menace in the sound of his words, which filled the room. "Will you allow me to search your memories?"

"They are not only mine. Roman, Daniel?" Grant asked, not taking his gaze away from the man in front of him.

"I have no problem if it helps him," Roman said, Grant next to him.

"Neither do I," Daniel added, leaning down and placing a kiss on her shoulder where the dress had slipped down to her arm.

A small shiver had Laura rubbing her arms and lifting her gaze to stare into Daniel's eyes, but as soon as his brother spoke, both turned to watch.

"Do it," Grant spoke as the man's hand came up.

"I am Gresan and my brother Evav. Thank you." Gresan placed the palm of his hand on Grant's forehead. A glowing light surrounded Grant and the other. Since both Daniel and Roman could read and communicate through their link, Daniel could actually feel the probe. Not only was this man looking for information about his brothers, but also trying to find out what happened to them those earlier years.

What seemed like 15 minutes only took five. Gresan released his brother and was once more beside his partner. "All of you have been wronged, as were our brothers. I'm sorry to cause you such grief. We did not mean to alarm you. We must take the news back to our home, but we would like permission to come back and teach you how to use some of your new abilities. But first I warn you." He looked at Grant, then at Roman, and finally at Daniel and Laura.

"You have not finished staking your claim on your woman. Do it now or the heat will be too strong later, and you might hurt her. Take the rest of the day and make her yours. Do not leave this room 'til the loop is complete. You'll know once it is, as will your men." Gresan lifted his hand, and Grant's hand, with the diamond on it, lifted as well.

"You have been chosen to be the leader of these people who have been harmed. I will warn you now, I sense others still out there. These things who did this to you and your brothers have not stopped." Gresan stopped as Evav began.

"Your compound here and the surrounding town will be fortified before we leave. Only those who mean you no harm may enter. Gresan forgot to mention one thing about the loop. Once it is done, your woman will need at least one of you near her. When your men or women find their mates, they too will need to stay close to their chosen ones. You have a word—sugar daddy, I believe?"

Laura stiffened in Daniel's arms, but at once he pulled her tighter against his body. "Shh, listen."

"This word might be offensive and I'm sorry to your woman for using it, but it is close to what will happen when the loop is finished. Not only will she need your touch, but your seed to survive. Each human who is joined with one of you will need this, even the female if she takes a male." The image of a man eating a woman's pussy appeared in his head. "He must make her release her juice and ingest it at least once a day." Evav cocked his head.

"We will explain more when we return in three of your Earth months. You will not be left alone. You are part of us now." With that, the two vanished from the room, but not before they announced the general had indeed been in on the experiments from the beginning and that he was now in the hands of two aliens who had just left.

"Well, that was interesting. Come on, everyone out. Alex, you grab Max and his diaper bag. We'll take care of him while these four take care of business," Nadine ordered, pushing the others out the door.

"Wait!" Laura leaned over and latched onto the

stroller, staring at Alex. "I've never been without Max longer than a few hours."

"Laura, look at me." Grant knelt next to them, placing his hands on her knees. "I know this asking a lot, but I promise we'll go down and get our supper later so you can see Max. Then Mom will have Alex back here first thing in the morning. If there are any problems, she'll come right to us."

"What if I can't do this? He said I could die, Grant. We were supposed to take this slow. I feel as if I'm being rushed into this. Plus, you're not really feeling anything of what he said, right?" Laura looked at Grant then at Roman.

"No, we don't, but should we risk it? We will check on Max throughout the night, but Mom is right. He needs to be with her and Alex so we can figure this out." Daniel ran his hands up and down Laura's arms.

"There is no going back. You are ours to love, to take care of and to spend the rest of our lives with. In some sense, Evav was right. We need to take care of you. It's not a compulsion. It's deeper." Grant took her hand and placed it over his heart.

"We are covering new territory here, but Daniel is right. We will not risk your health, but this has to be done."

"Hey guys, can you give me a little time with Laura?" Alex pushed in front of Roman and held out her hand to her friend. "We'll be right over there."

Knowing Daniel had no choice, he released her and helped her stand. Alex and Laura moved to the other side of the room, knowing they would be able to hear every word. Another one of their enhanced abilities, thanks to the general.

Chapter Fifteen

Wiping her hands on her dress, Laura took Alex's hand and allowed her to pull her to the other side of the room. "What the hell is going on with you? You accepted them earlier and now you're acting all skittish?" Alex hugged Laura tight before giving her the eye.

"Wouldn't you be scared? I mean come on, Alex. If they—my men—don't put their little guys in me I could die? I'm already craving their touch and just feeling their eyes on me has me hornier then a bitch in heat." She took a deep breath and tried to slow her breathing.

Alex frowned and reached up to place her hand on her forehead. "You are all flushed and sweaty." Her eyes got big. "What if you are feeling the effects? Maybe somehow the reverse is happening. Ever since earlier when you kissed Grant's hand…" She stopped and Laura nodded.

"That's it. I started something when I accepted him. Damn, now I can't even blame them," Laura teased and Alex grinned.

"Listen, I know this is way, way out there…but I don't get bad vibes about these guys. Your own mom came back and approved each one. You're the one who wanted the sugar daddy. Admit it, the thought of them taking care of you excites you because once you let go of all that excess baggage, you're going to shine, lady. You, of all people, deserve this." Her friend hugged her. "Max will be fine."

"What about you? Don't you think you do too?" Laura asked when she stepped away from her to leave.

"Hell yes I do, but now isn't my time. It's yours. Embrace it, and them." Alex said and squeezed her hand before turning to all three men. "If you hurt her, I swear I'll take a hunting knife to your balls."

Not even turning around, Laura headed for the bathroom and closed the door. She was sticky and needed a nice hot shower.

Music turned on in the outer room just before she reached over to turn on the water. She grinned listening to one of her favorite songs, "Beth," by Kiss. With the water at the perfect temp, Laura stripped out of her clothes, leaving them right where they fell.

The hot water eased the tension in her shoulder. She knew it was only a little after two in the afternoon, but Laura felt as if she'd pulled a double shift at work. Muscles ached along with something else. Laura didn't want to think of that right now, but it looked as if she had no choice.

Dunking her head under the water, she waited for whoever stepped into the bathroom. The rings on the shower curtain slid along the metal pole, but still Laura didn't open her eyes.

"Do you know how beautiful you look, standing there with the water rolling down your body?" Roman asked as he reached up and cupped her breasts.

My Sugar Daddy

In some ways, Roman was more like her than the others. His magic or both their ability to touch animals, gave them something Laura didn't have with the other brothers.

She lowered her head and opened her eyes to stare up at him. "We need you, Laura. There is no going back. Let us love you." Roman held her gaze even while he pinched and pulled at her nipples. "Reach up and hold onto the bar above you."

Forgetting about her injuries, Laura went to reach up and flinched when it pulled at her side. "Put your arms down. I'm sorry, baby. I totally forgot about your side. It won't happen again." He knelt before her and turned her so her injury was facing him. Carefully he removed the bandage.

"We'll wash this and let it air out now." Roman threw the bandage out of the tub and began to wash her. "I know you have questions and we'll answer them all." He stood and grabbed ahold of the showerhead.

"Face the wall and place your hands on it." He guided her into the position he wanted her. His cock brushed against her ass and Laura sucked in her breath. Daniel hadn't been wrong. Roman was hung like nothing she'd imagined.

"Shh, I'll take it slow when the time is right." Roman held the pulsing showerhead directly on her breast. Instead of multiple streams of water coming out, one strong one now teased her nipple.

From behind her, Roman slid his cock between her legs, rubbing her sensitive nether lips. She lowered her head watching as the tip of his cock peeked out between her legs.

"Roman..." She moaned and pushed against his chest with her back as he moved the water pressure to the other nipple.

"When you are completely healed, I have many things I want to do to you in this shower, but for now my brothers are waiting for us. Come." He stepped back, releasing her. The water turned off by itself and the shower curtain slid open. Grant was standing there.

"Come on, Laura, let's get you dried off." Grant held out his hand, but frowned at Roman. "Don't do that again. You are too close to losing it and you're not thinking straight," he snapped, shocking Laura.

"I'm fine, Grant, really." Laura tried to reassure him.

"I know you are, baby, or my brother would be sporting a nice black eye right about now." Grant took a large, warm towel and started to pat her dry. "It seems Evav was right about us—more so for Roman and you. You were right about the kiss to my hand. It did trigger something in each of us." Grant stood in front of her, so close her chest touched his.

"There is no turning back and I'm sorry we couldn't give you the time, but truthfully would you really have needed it?" Grant asked.

Daniel stood in the doorway, Roman behind her; the three of them waited. She took a deep breath. "No. I knew last night." Laura reached behind her and squeezed Roman's hand.

The three of them left the bathroom not touching or saying a word. Laura followed, unsure of what to do, but as soon as she stepped into their sitting room, there was no doubt.

"You're hurt, so we will have to be careful how

My Sugar Daddy

we take you." Grant stood by the bed while Roman crawled onto of it and lay down looking up at her. "Spread your legs, Laura. Allow Daniel and me to prepare you for Roman." Grant whispered as he threw Roman a tube of lubricant he took off a nearby table.

But what he took next had her trembling—a huge dildo. "This is the biggest I could find, it's a little wider than I am, but it will help spread you." He knelt in front of her and placed a kiss on her stomach. "Soon we'll shave you here." Grant cupped her mound while behind her Daniel squeezed her butt cheeks.

"I'm actually a little nervous." Laura smiled as she reached up and brushed a single stray piece of his dark hair out of his face. "I'll need you for the rest of my life to survive, but what if you get tired of me? What if I don't please you anymore or meet your needs? I'm only one," she whispered and swallowed.

"There is no other for us Laura. You are it. When I touch you, smell you and taste you, it's like nothing I've ever experienced. You're our light, you make everything right again." Grant slid two lubed fingers into her and she reached out holding onto his shoulders.

"We only see you," Daniel said as his fingers slid into her ass. "We belong to each other."

"Spread your legs a little further," Grant tapped the inside of her thigh before he inched the silicone phallus into her channel slowly.

"God, that feels good—more please," Laura moaned. She had never been more turned on. She was so wet that the insides of her thighs were damp. Her nipples hardened to points as both Grant and Daniel worked her body into a frenzy.

"You're doing so good, baby, but now it's time." Grant pulled out the toy and threw it to the corner, before helping her up onto the bed. "Take him into you, Laura. You can do it."

Crawling up Roman's body, Laura stared into his face as she leveled herself over him. "You are so handsome," she said, sliding her finger down the side of his face. He turned and nipped her finger and she laughed.

Roman held onto her hips as Laura took ahold of his well-lubed cock and guided the tip of it to her pussy lips. He was so thick Laura couldn't close her hand totally around him.

She knew this was going to hurt, but the pain would only add to her pleasure, she hoped.

Daniel handed Grant the lube while he watched Laura take his brother inch by inch. Daniel was so hard he was having a hard time controlling the urge to join them, but it was not time yet.

"Almost there, Laura," Roman grunted out, but lost it at the last minute, surging up into her and causing her to scream.

"Roman!" she held on to his shoulders. Tears slid down her cheeks. "Don't move."

Daniel moved with Grant to the bed, petting and kissing Laura while glaring at Roman. "You are doing great, Laura. God, you look so sexy with his cock buried inside you." Daniel nibbled the side of her neck while Grant took her nipple into his mouth.

Slowly, Laura pushed herself up and slid back down. A little moan escaped and they knew it was time. Releasing her breast, Grant moved behind her, guiding her body down on Roman. "Rest your head on his chest, baby, and try to relax as much as possible.

This is going to be tight, but it has to be." His brothers moaned together and Daniel knew Grant had slid past the tight ring of her ass.

Gripping his dick, Daniel stroked it while watching and waiting. Laura's whimpers and cries only increased his sexual appetite.

"I'm in," Grant grunted and slid partway out. "Lift your head, baby, and take Daniel's cock. He's waited long enough for that warm mouth."

Not wasting any time, Daniel crawled onto the side of the bed. Her big eyes focused on his cock. Seeing the drop of his seed on the tip Daniel rubbed it on her lips, wetting them. "Open for me, Laura. Give me some of that hot loving." She smiled and licked the top of his penis, teasing.

"Laura, I'm too close," he snarled and grabbed a handful of her hair, trying to guide her.

Opening her mouth, Laura took him in as far as she could. At the same time, Grant threw open the link to each of them.

Sweat dripped down his chest and face as his balls tightened while Daniel fucked her mouth. "Not going to last," Daniel warned and his brothers grunted.

Her body begun to shake and strange light seemed to burst from her as all four of them groaned together. His seed shot down her throat as an orgasm hit her fast and hard.

With one last pump, Daniel released his hold on her head and slid his cock out of her mouth just in time to hear her shout.

"What the hell?" Laura sat up quick knocking her head into Grant's chin as her hands flew to her neck. "It burns!"

Trinity Blacio

He was up next to her in seconds. "What's wrong? Move your hands, Laura. Let us see what's happening." Daniel tried to pull her hands away, while Grant slid out of her and Roman sat up, holding onto her.

"It hurts," she cried again. Her lips trembled, but finally Laura removed her fingers. Red diamond shapes about an inch long formed a circle around her neck, matching the one on his hand.

Grant got up and ran into the bathroom bringing out a washcloth. "This is cold, baby. It might help with the burning." He wrapped it around her neck and looked at him.

"It's getting better, but what is it? Why are you three staring at me?" Daniel smiled and cupped her cheek.

"You carry my brother's mark now," Roman said kissing her lips and lifting her off him. She moaned and frowned at the same time.

"Wait, what happened to the staples?" Laura looked down at her side, his gaze following hers. Every staple was gone and she was totally healed. "Wow, you guys have some powerful little guys there," Laura teased, running her fingers over the small scar. "I feel different too." She cocked her head. "The loop is finished, I believe, but there is something that still needs to be done. It's weird—it feels like a pull, as if I need to be somewhere." Laura moved to the bathroom and they followed her, afraid she would hate the marking.

"Red is my favorite color and I always wanted a tattoo." She tilted her head to one side, then the other. "I wonder if this will happen to the others of your

My Sugar Daddy

team. We need to write these questions down to ask the next time Evav and his brother come."

Taking a towel, Grant placed a kiss on her cheek. "That will be your job. Daniel, Roman, they're waiting."

At once an image appeared in Daniel's head and he snarled. "She's not going to like it," he muttered and moved back into the sitting room to grab his pants.

"Like what and why are you three putting pants on? Are you done with me already?" She pouted following him into the room.

Going into their bedroom, Grant spoke forcefully. "No, were far from finished with you, lady, but first you need to be introduced to our family." He came back holding a red silk robe.

"Why do I have wear that? I have my clothes." Laura eyed Grant and waited.

"Are you going to question me all the time?" His brother asked holding her gaze 'til she looked down at the ground and sighed.

"No." She turned, putting her arm into the robe.

"I'm not going to lie. What is about to happen will be uncomfortable for us all, but it must be done even though it will never take place again."

"Maybe I should clean up first?" She asked.

"No, they need to smell us on you. These men and women will protect you with their lives. It seems we can't live too far apart. We'll always need to touch base every few weeks. Another aspect of the general's sick experiment," Grant snarled. "If that man were still here, I'd rip him apart."

Stepping in front of them, Daniel reached up and flicked the switch, opening the hidden tunnel. He stepped back and allowed his brother to guide Laura through the entrance.

This not only led to an outside vent, but to another section Roman had built over the last few years. Where only those who had been experimented on knew of.

Ahead of him, Daniel watched as Laura rubbed her arms. "Hold on, Grant, let me get some slippers and a blanket for her." He turned and ran back, grabbing the slippers and a blanket off their bed.

Daniel knelt down in front of Laura. "Give me your foot, Laura. We don't need you to catch a cold." Her foot was small in his hand as he put the slipper on it. "These will at least keep your feet warm."

"Thank you," Laura said. She reached up and kissed his lips as he wrapped the blanket around her shoulders.

"There is no need to thank me. We'll always take care of you." He tapped her nose and stood back.

"Come, they are waiting for us." Grant waited 'til Laura stepped up to his side before wrapping his arm around her waist. He released the magic that kept his true color of his skin, as did Daniel.

There was no reason to hide, since every person waiting for them would also be in their natural state.

Chapter Sixteen

Even with a blanket wrapped around her, Laura was still cold. She watched Grant's expressions play on his face as they walked down the tunnel. Nothing. Laura could tell nothing. Whereas Daniel's reactions were always all-telling.

He looked down at her and smiled. "Don't worry, Laura, we'll be right beside you the whole time." Grant ran his hand up and down her back.

"You going to tell me what they're going to do?" she asked, but he shook his head and reached for the metal door.

"When we're done here, I'm taking you back to our room and locking the doors," Grant's heated gaze met hers before it traveled down her body slowly. "Being a leader can suck some days and this is one of those days." He shoved the door open.

More than 100 men and a few women stood around a small stage in the middle of the room. Laura couldn't comprehend how someone could have experimented on so many people without being caught.

Bringing her attention back into focus, Laura scanned the room. On the stage was what looked like a lounging chair. The crowd parted as Grant led her to the bottom of the stage.

The room was warm and all eyes were on her. Grant turned to her. "I need the robe and blanket, Laura." He held out his hand and waited.

She sucked in her breath, looking at Daniel then at Roman. Neither of them said a word as they waited and watched.

Releasing the blanket, Laura placed it over Grant's arm, but removing the robe was harder. With her stomach in her throat, she slipped it off staring down at the ground as she handed it to Grant.

Thankful the room was warmer than the tunnel, Laura crossed her arms over her breasts, but all too soon Grant pried her arms away. "You are too beautiful to hide," he said. He once more placed his arm around her waist and escorted her up the stairs. Grant leaned down and kissed her cheek. "Do you trust me?" She nodded.

"Good." He turned and sat down in the lounger, his legs splayed. He patted the spot in between his legs. "Come sit."

She eyed him and the chair for a few seconds before mumbling. "Payback is a bitch, remember that." Laura crawled onto the lounger, resting her back against Grant's chest crossing her legs in front of her, hoping not to flash everyone…She stiffened suddenly, a picture in her head. "NO!" Laura tried to sit up, but Grant closed his arms around her and held her tight.

"One time, each member of my team needs to know you. When it's done, we'll go to our room and I'll show you how proud I am of you."

"Who gives a shit if you're proud of me? I can't

My Sugar Daddy

do this," Laura snapped, but inside, she wanted him to be proud of her. Roman and Daniel knelt on either side of the chair.

"Yes. you can. You are one of the strongest people I know. Who else could have held her head up and started all over after all the trouble that prick Warren caused? You are their queen now, Laura. They need to pay homage to you. It's the others' way," Roman said, sliding his hand up the inside of her leg his fingers brushing against her pussy lips.

"Do you know the most beautiful and precious spot on a women's body is her pussy?" Daniel asked as he reached over and lifted her stiff leg. He kissed the inside of her knee before placing it on his side of the chair, opening her to their view. "It gives her man pleasure and it is the place where their child is conceived. It's also one of the most sensitive parts on her body. What better place to kiss?"

Laura knew what they were doing and was really trying not to freak out. Grant cupped her breasts, while Roman slid his finger in and out of her. "Your scent is intoxicating to us," he mumbled before placing a kiss on her lips and turning as the first man, Seth stepped up to the lounger and knelt between her legs.

"Thank you for taking our leader into you, for giving him light when there seemed to be nothing but darkness." He kissed her pussy lips then her mouth before leaving to allow the next in line to do the same.

For the next hour, everyone on their team came up and pledged themselves, even the women. In some ways it was beautiful, but toward the end Laura noticed how much this had truly affected her men.

Daniel was stiff beside her. His grip on the side of

the lounger would have crushed her bones if he had been holding onto her. Laura had to hide her smile twice when a man came up and she heard Roman's quiet snarl. Each man had nodded to Roman, but continued their pledge.

Behind her, Grant was stiff as a board. Several times he hissed in her ear, but he never moved. When the last man moved down the stairs, Grant stood and looked around the room. "Thank you all. Now, if you will excuse us, we will take our woman back to our room. Seth, I want a report. If anything changes, Zenith, make sure Alex is protected and that she wants for nothing while we are busy." With that, a cheer went up and she found herself up over Grant's shoulder, his hand on her ass.

She laughed as he ran down the stairs with Daniel and Roman right behind them. Laura placed her hands on Grant's back and lifted up. "Are we in hurry for something?"

The three of them snarled, but Grant slapped her ass hard. "Wait!"

In a matter of minutes, Grant was strolling into their room and tossing her down on the bed. The three of them stood around the bed, stripping out of their pants. Their cocks were hard. Each one started to stroke their huge members while watching her. It was one of the sexiest and most beautiful things she'd ever seen.

"Open your legs and pull them up toward your chest. Let us see all of you," Grant ordered and stepped aside as Daniel crawled in between her legs.

"It's going to be quick and hard," Daniel gritted out before sliding his cock into her in one stroke.

Even after having Roman in her, Daniel was big. Going from no sex to all the sex she needed was going to take some time getting used to. With Grant on one side and Roman on the other, they both took a breast into their palms, squeezing. As if they'd choreographed it, the brothers lowered their heads at the same time and sucked her nipples into their mouths.

"Damn!" Laura lost it and grabbed onto the sheet under her.

Wetting one of his fingers, Grant reached under her and pushed his finger into her ass. Hands, mouths, lips—the sensations were too much as Daniel pumped in and out.

She'd have bruises in the morning, but that was fine by her. Her toes curled and she grabbed onto Grant's and Roman's heads. The second orgasm of the day ripped through her quick and fast.

Daniel joined her, his seed emptying into her body. He snarled and thrust one more time before sliding out.

Not giving her any time to recuperate, Grant took Daniel's place. "Wrap your legs around my waist and hold onto my neck," he ordered, sliding inside her and picking her up off the bed.

He didn't go far, as her back hit the wall with a thud. "Sorry, must have you. No one…" he snarled as his gaze held hers. "No one will ever touch you again."

She smiled and placed both of her hands on his face. "Only you three. I don't need any others. Love me, Grant, just love me."

"Always," he mumbled. As his mouth covered

hers, a third orgasm hovered close. All it would take was one…stroke.

"Grant!" Laura broke the kiss, her nails digging into his shoulder. Her shaking legs fell open as he thrust into her twice more. His seed mixed with Daniel's and ran down her leg.

Strong arms scooped her up when Grant pulled out of her. "Come on, baby, let's take a nice hot bath," Roman whispered in her hair. He carried her into the bathroom and placed her on the counter while he checked the temperature of the water.

"After we clean you up, we'll go eat and you can see Max before we retire for the night," Roman promised; she whimpered when he picked her back up.

"Relax, I can wait. I just want to take care of you." He stepped into the water holding her and carefully sat down.

Laura moaned as the water eased the ache between her legs. "You'll heal fast with our seed inside you now." Roman picked up a sponge, soaped it up and slowly ran it over her skin.

"It's not going to be easy, Laura. All three of us are very possessive and tend to act first and ask questions later. But I do promise you and Max will want for nothing and no one could love you more than us."

Running the sponge between her legs, Laura tried to grab his hand. "Easy. I just want to clean you." His voice was low and smooth.

She released his hand and settled against his chest. Laura slowly opened her legs for him. "Aren't you scared, Roman, not knowing what to expect?"

"No, because I have my family and now you, plus

I'm not the only one in the same boat. We have each other. We'll make mistakes and there will be things we won't like, but when it comes down to it, nothing matters as long as you are beside us and safe. Before, there was only darkness on some days, but now we have hope because of you."

"Roman, I'm not a miracle worker." Laura kissed the side of his neck and relaxed. Finally seeing where she fit in their lives.

"Mom and Alex are here with supper and Max," Grant announced from the door. With his black jeans on and his shirt only buttoned halfway Laura smiled.

Oh yes, Laura was indeed lucky. There was a lot of unknown, but her sugar daddies would always place her needs first and what else could a woman want or need. She reached up and ran her hand over the marking. Laura was truly collared and loved it.

Excerpt from

Secrets Unwrapped
Book Two of the Sugar Daddies Series

Big Beautiful Women *is a website for servicemen.*

"We're looking for that special lady. You will be spoiled and cared for. Do you dare take the chance and register? Who knows what will be beyond that next click?"

A dating website set up by the Wilmot brothers as a backup warning system. A network that only military-families have access to. Not even the government could break through their security, but no one thought that it would be one of the only systems still working in the next few months. And the world as they had known it was now gone.

Chapter One

Blood covered her hands, shoes and aching body. Alex Martin knew her ankle was badly twisted, at the very least. Her finger was broken, along with maybe a few ribs, but she was alive. Her ears still rang from the fatal gunshot that was responsible for the bullet wound in her attacker's head.

What she had done had been the only way to stop the man from killing her and the baby she carried. Alex closed her eyes, and leaned her head against the wall. She tried to remember something to make her smile.

Her lip hurt, but she did smile, remembering that first night she'd been with her three men. They were hers, Bo, Rafe and Justin. She lifted her hand and placed it on her lower belly.

"I don't want to be alone, please hold me," Alex had begged Bo. She knew he was the one that always made the decisions for the group.

He cupped her face before kissing her lips softly. "If we stay, I can't promise we'll be gentlemen."

"Why would I want gentlemen?" Alex teased, hoping he would get the hint. She needed them holding her and if it led to something else, so be it. Alex had

never had a one-night stand, but these men were well worth it. Who could pass up having three men touching every inch of your body? Plus, it took her mind off the anniversary of the death of her son, six years ago.

The first clue that they were staying was when Bo lifted his T-shirt up over his head. "Rafe, Alex is wearing too many clothes, why don't you help her strip. After all, it's going to get a little warm in here." And boy had he been right.

Opening her eyes, Alex shivered at the blood splattered around her. She had tried using her knife three times. Alex had stabbed her assailant while he choked and punched her, but it was as if he'd been on some kind of drug. He kept hitting her, so she'd grabbed hold of his pistol and shot him. Rising to her feet, Alex tucked the gun into the back of her pants. She scanned the area around her, making sure there were no other attackers.

Not seeing anyone else, Alex started on her trip back towards the main tunnel. Her ankle killing her, Alex limped down the smaller, older tunnel she'd found an hour ago. Her hand automatically rubbed her belly, and she shivered. Alex remembered the one time Bo had taken her hard and fast, before they had been interrupted.

"Bo does not like to be teased..." she laughed, but inside Alex wished for his arms around her right now.

Not even her best friend Laura knew that she was carrying Bo's baby. Alex had had all the signs of pregnancy - she'd missed her monthly and her breasts were tender. One thing that had always been certain in her life was the bloody curse women everywhere got.

Secrets Unwrapped

She just hoped that side hit to the ribs didn't damage anything or hurt her baby.

With Laura busy with her men, and their mother Nadine taking care of Laura's son Max, Alex had become bored and lonely. She so wanted to see Rafe, Bo and Justin. Not to mention give them a piece of her mind, leaving her like they had. Not just for a damn week, a very long month had gone by. Alex still couldn't get their faces out of her head or the memory of their touch.

Right now, she sure wouldn't mind having them around. Alex wanted Bo to know he was going to be a father before she told anyone. Alex snorted. Who the hell was she kidding? In that one night, the big jerks had formed a circle around her heart, claiming it as theirs. But could they work through the extra emotional baggage she carried?

Patting her belly, Alex whispered. "Maybe it's a sign. Telling me it's time to move on."

Laura handled her problems. It was time for Alex to do the same with hers. But there was that doubt that grew inside her. Would they even welcome a child?

And what of the child? She'd been there when the aliens had come. When they'd told Grant and the rest of them that they carried alien DNA. Bo carried alien DNA. Her child carried alien DNA. What would that do to her?

Hearing footsteps, Alex pulled out the gun, dropped into a crouch, and waited. Even though the sounds were coming from the tunnels she had recently walked through, she damn well wasn't going to take anything for granted. She'd be ready if anyone else tried to kill her or the baby again today. With her hands shaking, Alex waited.

"Alex, where are you?" Daniel yelled.

A small cry escaped her as she dropped the gun and slid to the floor.

"Here," she whispered, waiting for her friends. Resting her head against the wall, Alex watched Daniel, Seth, and Torch come around the corner to stand in front of her.

"What happened, Pretty Lady?" Seth asked, kneeling down and taking in her appearance.

Pointing down the tunnel, she reported, "He came out of nowhere. At first I thought he was part of your group, that's when he first hit me. I tried to stop him. I think I shot him. He was too big and he just kept coming," her voice squeaked and she started to shake. "So cold," her voice was jittery.

"She's going into shock, " Seth said. "I have to get her back to the tunnels under the compound." He reached under her and carefully picked her up. But even that little movement hurt and she whimpered.

"Ribs hurt." Alex rested her head on Seth's shoulder.

"Laura is going to have a fit. I want to know why this tunnel wasn't sealed off and who that is down there," Daniel ordered. Ten other men came running with weapons drawn.

Daniel looked down at her as they made their way back to the newer tunnels. "What were you doing down there, Alex? You could have been killed," he shoved open a door. Roman stood waiting for them with Laura.

"Alex!" her friend cried.

"I'm fine. Just a few broken bones, I think. I'll be okay," she tried to reassure her friend, but was just so tired.

Secrets Unwrapped

"Don't you go to sleep on me yet Alex," Seth said. "Answer Daniel's questions." He seemed to be moving faster toward what was now the medical center for the compound.

"I was bored. I went exploring. I didn't think that there would be anything dangerous down here... I just wanted to see them. I needed to talk with Bo. Stupid, I know. Should make them come back to me. Never again, stupid men," she groaned. "He ruined my favorite jeans." She tried not to cry, but the tears rolled down her cheeks.

Reaching the medical unit, Seth laid her onto the hospital bed.

"Sweetie, I'm going to have to take these bloody things off now. I need to see where you're hurt," Seth mumbled. His gaze traveled down her body trying to assess the damage.

She nodded, not caring if anyone could see her fat black body. "Whatever, but be warned, there's a lot of fat." She tried to close her eyes, but once again Seth stopped that.

"Oh, no you don't. Keep those beautiful eyes on me, pretty lady. And you're not fat. You're beautiful, round in all the right places." He ripped her shirt right down the middle with his bare hands, shocking her with his strength.

"Wow, impressive." She wiggled her eyebrows and he laughed. Alex turned to see Laura standing there, smiling and shaking her head.

"Why didn't you come and get me?" Laura asked, taking her hand.

"You are lucky she didn't or I'd be beating your ass," Roman grumbled and moved into the hallway as

Seth stripped Alex of her clothes. Only Laura and Seth were in the room when the door flew open and Nadine rushed in.

"What the hell happened?" With her hands on her hips, she looked at Alex. "You know better than going off by yourself. You should have taken one of us with you." Nadine had repeated what Laura had said and Seth snorted.

"None of you should be going anywhere without an escort. Until this threat is gone you need to be more careful," Seth said. He threw her clothes into the trash while covering her with a paper-like blanket. "I'm going to get some warm water and clean you up so I can see where you are hurt, but can you give me a general idea here what I'm dealing with?"

"First tell me why in the hell every hospital has to have these paper blankets? They don't keep anything warm," she snapped and fidgeted with it. "Laura, make a list. New blankets for this place. I have a broken finger, maybe a few ribs on my side and I think I sprained my ankle. Oh, and my head is killing me. Got any aspirin? Wait! Forget that, can't have aspirin now.," she rambled on and he shook his head.

"No aspirin until I find out what all is wrong. Why can't you have any? Are you allergic to anything?" he asked, turning to the cupboard. He grabbed what appeared to be a bucket, and filled it with water.

"No," she sighed and looked back at Laura. "At least I get a sponge bath from a hot man," she tried to joke around.

Both Laura and Nadine snorted. "You have no shame, you hussy," Laura kissed the side of her head. "Don't do this again. I can't lose you Alex."

"Hey, you're not going to lose me. You know I'm a tough bird. Plus, I was doing what you said." Alex really wished she could just go back to her room and curl up in her own bed. Her ribs were starting to throb.

"What did I say?" Laura asked while Seth proceeded to wash her down. He started at her feet, checking on her ankle.

"Damn, that hurts," Alex tried to move away from his probing hands, but her ribs stopped her movements instantly. "I'm so going to kill those three jerks. Oh no, they had to go play hero, damn it. Remember, no shots or pills... baby." She looked at Laura, but the room was getting darker. "Who's playing with..."

About the Author

Trinity Blacio is the # 1 Amazon bestselling romance writer of such paranormal erotic romance series as the *Running in Fear* and *Masters of the Cats* series, as well as a number of dark fantasy, erotic romance, erotic horror and ménage titles. She is a PAN member of the Ohio chapter of Romance Writers of America and is the bestselling author of a paranormal stepbrothers series that made her an All Romance eBooks and Siren bestselling author.

Coming from a split family, Trinity Blacio has lived in Minnesota, California, Michigan, Florida, but eventually settled in the state where she was born—Ohio. She has an Associate's Degree in Psychology and Social Work from Lorain County Community College and a Bachelor's Degree in Psychology from Cleveland State University.

You will find her on Facebook, Twitter and Goodreads. She loves to talk with all her fans.

Other Riverdale Avenue Titles by Trinity Blacio

Secrets Unwrapped: Sugar Daddies

* * *

The Running in Fear Series

Searching for the Perfect Mate: Remi's Story Prequel to The Running in Fear Series

Escaped: Book One of the Running in Fear Series

Abandoned: Book Two of Running in Fear

* * *

The Stepbrothers Series

Her Stepbrothers' Demands

Her Stepbrothers are Aliens

Her Stepbrothers are Demons

Her Stepbrothers are Blood Suckers

Her Stepbrothers are Dragons

Her Stepbrothers are Saber Tooth Tigers
Book Five of The Masters of the Cats Series

Her Stepbrothers are Werewolves

The Virgin Witch and the Vampire King

* * *

The Virgin Witch and the Vampire King
Book One: Wedding Bells Times Four

The Virgin Witch and the Vampire King
Book Two: Training a Wife

* * *

Masters of the Cats: Collaring the Saber-Tooth, Book One

Masters of the Cats: Dee's Hard Limits, Book Two

Masters of the Cats: Caging the Bengal Tiger, Book Three

A Christmas Tail: Book Four of the Masters of the Cats Series

* * *

Surrender Your Independence

Red Satin Lips: Book One of The Surrender Series

* * *

*The Naughty Angel and Her Three Very Wise men
Book in The Naughty Series*

*Naughty Mommy and Santa's Helpers
Book Two of the Naughty Series*

*The Naughty Stepbrothers
Book Three of The Naughty Series*

* * *

*Jeanne-Claude and Eugene's Magic Lamp
Books One: I Dream of Jinns*

Hot for Winter: A Christmas Ménage

Embracing the Winds

Stoned Love

Her Three Men

Possession of the Soul: Book One of The Fantasy is Alive Series

I Left My Heart in Sin City

The Empress' Rapture

Three in a Bed
A Collection of Ménage Novellas by Joy Daniels,
Louisa Bacio and Trinity Blacio

Made in the USA
San Bernardino, CA
11 June 2017